There was something in Alexandra's eyes that
warned Robert she was afraid of getting hurt.
Something that warned him it would be like coaxing a wild creature to get her to trust him. And
some answering spark in his own breast that told
him he would, he must, find a way to do so.

"You needn't be afraid of me," he said softly.
"This is madness, I know, and in the morning perhaps we both shall regret such madness. But right
now, in this moment, I cannot bring myself to do
so."

And then, before Miss Barlow could protest, indeed before Robert even truly knew himself what
he intended, he leaned forward and kissed her on
the lips. And it was as sweet as anything he could
have imagined. . . .

The Ambitious Baronet

April Kihlstrom

A SIGNET BOOK

SIGNET
Published by New American Library, a division of
Penguin Putnam Inc., 375 Hudson Street,
New York, New York 10014, U.S.A.
Penguin Books Ltd, 27 Wrights Lane,
London W8 5TZ, England
Penguin Books Australia Ltd, Ringwood,
Victoria, Australia
Penguin Books Canada Ltd, 10 Alcorn Avenue,
Toronto, Ontario, Canada M4V 3B2
Penguin Books (N.Z.) Ltd, 182–190 Wairau Road,
Auckland 10, New Zealand

Penguin Books Ltd, Registered Offices:
Harmondsworth, Middlesex, England

First published by Signet, an imprint of New American Library,
a division of Penguin Putnam Inc.

First Printing, March 2001
10 9 8 7 6 5 4 3 2 1

 REGISTERED TRADEMARK—MARCA REGISTRADA

Printed in the United States of America

PUBLISHER'S NOTE
This is a work of fiction. Names, characters, places, and incidents either are
the product of the author's imagination or are used fictitiously, and any
resemblance to actual persons, living or dead, business establishments,
events, or locales is entirely coincidental.

BOOKS ARE AVAILABLE AT QUANTITY DISCOUNTS WHEN USED TO PROMOTE
PRODUCTS OR SERVICES. FOR INFORMATION PLEASE WRITE TO PREMIUM
MARKETING DIVISION, PENGUIN PUTNAM INC., 375 HUDSON STREET, NEW
YORK, NEW YORK 10014.

Prologue

Miss Alexandra Barlow, daughter to Lord Henley, liked children. She truly did. But the woman in the woods, Margaret, had a way of turning up with them and expecting Miss Barlow to deal with the resulting problem. Today she had something else in mind as well.

Alex stared at the older woman before her and frowned. "M-my m-m-mother gave you something for me?" she stammered. "Why did you never say so before?"

The woman shrugged. "There was no point to it. She gave me this for you and said that I should hold it until I felt you had need of it."

"Need?"

Margaret didn't answer. Instead, she handed the younger woman a locket. It was old and intricately engraved. On the back was a tiny inscription. Alex read it aloud.

" 'Wish Always with Love.' What does that mean?"

"It is all foolishness," Margaret replied brusquely. "But you are supposed to wish for what you want most in your life, and then open the locket. It's all nonsense, but I suppose you may as well do it."

Alex closed her eyes and thought about the dreams she'd always had. When she opened her eyes, she opened the locket as well, and, for a brief moment, a man's face appeared. It was not precisely a handsome face, but there was something in his eyes that seemed to reach into her soul.

And then, abruptly, the image disappeared. Alex blinked. She looked again. Nothing. The locket was empty. She closed the locket and opened it again. Still nothing.

"What was that?" she murmured and looked to Margaret for answers.

But the older woman merely turned away and pretended to be studying one of the containers of herbs on her shelf. "Nonsense," she muttered to herself. "It's all nonsense."

"What is nonsense?" Alex persisted.

Margaret hesitated, then turned to face her. With more than a little exasperation in her voice she said, "When you hold the locket for the first time, you are supposed to wish for your heart's desire and then, when you open it, you are supposed to see the face of the man you ought to marry. It is a ridiculous legend, that's all. There must be some trick of how it's made that makes one think one sees a face."

That made sense. But another thought occurred to Alex and she asked, "If this was my mother's locket, why didn't she give it to me before she died? And what do you mean that you felt I had need of it?"

But Margaret merely shook her head. "Did I say need? I meant that she trusted me to give it to you when you were grown up, and at five-and-twenty I should think you are ready to take care of it properly. And now no more foolish questions. You must return home." The older woman paused and inclined her head toward the basket Alex had brought. "I thank you for your kindness."

"And I thank you for yours," Alex countered, looking toward the child who played so happily in the dirt at their feet. "I will take him to the village with me. The blacksmith and his wife have long been wishing for a child."

Impulsively, Margaret reached out and took Alexandra's hand in hers. "You will have children of your own, someday!" she said fiercely.

Alex shook her head. "No. Despite the face I thought I saw in the locket, I will never marry. I know that, have known that, for some time now. Sometimes I wish, yes, I wish with all my heart that I could. But it does not matter. I have grown accustomed to my fate."

Was it only her imagination that the locket in her hand seemed to grow warm? It must be, Alex told herself. Such things didn't happen. And it had been, it must have been, only her imagination that made her think she saw a face.

But Margaret was speaking again. "It matters," she said dryly. "And you will marry. You must not become a foolish old spinster like me!"

Alex only shook her head again. She gathered up her cloak and the child, saying soothingly, "Come, it is time to find you a new home. I know just the one for you. You will like the blacksmith and his wife. I promise you will."

The child made no protest, and Alex wondered where he had come from, what his life had been like. But these were questions she had promised Margaret not to ask. All she needed to know was that he needed a new home. And then his shirt slipped free of the ragged pants and she could see the bruises up and down his back. Alex drew in her breath. There was no need to ask anything now for she had all the answer she could have wanted. Once more the older woman had rescued a child, and once more she had turned to Alex to help her find that child a new home.

Neither of them feared angry parents would come looking for the child. They never did. Not here, anyway. Not the children who came to Margaret.

As they walked to the village, Alex kept expecting the child to tell her he was tired, but not a word of complaint passed his lips. Indeed, no words did so. He was utterly silent, and if she had not heard him speak to the older woman, Alexandra would have wondered if he were mute.

When they reached the village, more than one
friendly smile greeted them, but no one came toward
Alex. They knew her too well, she thought grimly.
They knew that she would be looking for someone to
take in the child. And none of them wished to offer
him a home. Well, it did not matter. The new blacksmith and his wife would surely be happy to see her.
It was all the woman could talk about, her desire for
a child and her sorrow over her barren circumstance.

At the smithy, however, Alex received a severe set-
back. She was not greeted with the open arms she
expected. "What do you be wanting?" the smith demanded, not even looking up from his work.

"I-I brought a child. I know your wife has been
wanting one, and this child needs a home."

She gently pushed the child forward, but still the
smith did not look at him. From the doorway, a voice
said, "I-I've changed my mind."

Alexandra turned and froze as she saw the bruise
on the woman's face. Immediately, Alex grasped the
child and pulled him back to her. "I, that is, never
mind. I have another home for the child anyway."

"Good," the smith said.

The woman merely turned her face away, a streak
of tears on her bruised cheek.

And that was how Alex came to have the first child
in her care. She had wished for children, it was true,
but this was not quite what she had had in mind. How
on earth was she going to hide him when Papa came
home again?

In London, two men, David Thornsby and Sir Robert Stamford, stared at each other across a desk.

"Children are disappearing," Thornsby said bluntly.
"We've had a dozen complaints in the last six months
alone. All in the same region of the country. We want
you to find out what's going on."

"Whose children?" Stamford asked, his voice and
face as serious as the other man's.

Thornsby waved a hand carelessly. "Apprentices. Children from the mills and the mines. A parent or two has reported a child missing as well. We managed to find out that they were all being taken or sent to this village."

He pointed to a spot on a map. Stamford peered at it. "By whom were they being taken or sent there and why?"

"We don't know. Our source of information abruptly disappeared. But the last time such a thing happened, the children were being sold to a ring of men and ended up, after they were done with them, in brothels in London. The ones who survived, that is."

"And you think that is happening again?"

"That or worse," Thornsby agreed. "And I want you to find the men doing this and stop them."

"Shall I go directly to this village?" Stamford asked.

"First I'd like you to cultivate Lord Henley," Thornsby said slowly. "I don't much like the man myself. He is far too fond of gambling. But he may have seen or heard something. In any event, an invitation to stay at his home there would be invaluable. You'd provoke far less suspicion, be far less likely to frighten off our quarry, if you appear to be merely one more of Henley's foolish friends from London. And if he is involved, he may betray himself to you while you are there."

Stamford nodded. He rose to his feet and replied, "I am already somewhat acquainted with Henley. I dislike the man, but I shall do what I can to make him think me a friend. It shouldn't be difficult. As you say, he likes to gamble. All I need do is engage him in a game or two."

Chapter 1

The three Barlow sisters made a pretty picture as they sat in the sunny parlor at the front of their house. The eldest, Alexandra, was engaged in mending sheets and shirts and socks and such. Theresa, second eldest, was writing a long letter to their father. And the youngest, Elizabeth, was reading. All very typical for this household. Placed as they were so far from any town, there was not a great deal to do, and they had long since learned the art of entertaining themselves and one another.

Their greatest outside excitement came from the occasional visit from the vicar or a tenant—or the even more occasional visit from their father, when he could tear himself away from the delights of London. That, however, had come to be their greatest dread. So now, when the knocking sounded at the front door below them, they looked at one another with alarm.

"The children are napping," Tessa said.

"And Betsy will know to keep them quiet," Alex added. "I wonder how long Papa means to stay this time."

"Far too long if he's gambled away this quarter's rents again," Lisbeth asserted bitterly.

"More likely he is simply running from some woman's husband," Tessa countered. "One must hope that this time the fellow doesn't follow him here! I shall never forget the sight of Father crouched on the stair telling us to deny to the man that he was here."

"Don't even jest about such things!" Alex scolded.

Even as her sisters muttered that jesting was the furthest thing from their minds, the parlor door opened and Potter announced that Mr. James was here.

A small man with pinched features entered the room. He stared at the sisters with what could only be called a disapproving air, and his eyes took in the shabby state of the furnishings.

His inspection roused Alexandra's ire. Her chin came up in unconscious defiance. "May we help you, sir?" she asked, a decided chill in her voice. "Unfortunately my father is not much at home these days. And if you are a creditor, you had best apply to him in London for payment. We have no funds to do so."

He blinked at her. "Do you not know who I am?" he asked, patently taken aback.

"Ought we to know you?" Alex countered, though her tone softened just a trifle.

A thin smile crossed his lips, then quickly vanished. "No, how should you?" he admitted. "I merely thought that perhaps your father might, upon some occasion, have mentioned the name of his solicitor."

"His solicitor!"

The man turned to bow toward Tessa, who was the one who had echoed his words. "Yes, your father's solicitor," he repeated. "I presume I have the honor of addressing Miss Barlow and her two sisters."

"You do," Alex agreed.

He turned back to her, opened his mouth, and hesitated. "May I sit down?" he asked.

Alex flushed. "Yes. Yes, of course, sir. My apologies for keeping you standing!"

"Oh, I quite understand, if you thought I was a creditor!"

The stranger's eyes twinkled as he spoke, and Alex found herself feeling much more kindly toward him. "Would you care for tea? Or some other refreshment?" she asked. "I must presume you have come a long way, perhaps even from London if you are my father's solicitor."

He hesitated. "Perhaps later," he said. "For now, well, this is not a pleasant business, and I should dislike to put it off any longer."

"Of course."

Still he hesitated. Still he fiddled with his spectacles. But finally he looked at each of the sisters in turn and then looked at the eldest.

"There is no easy way to say this. Your father is dead."

He waited for their cries of surprise and was surprised himself when there were none. It was the youngest, Lisbeth, who answered his unspoken question.

"I suppose some angry husband shot Father in a duel?"

"No, no, nothing of the sort!" he hastened to assure her. And then he found himself at a loss for words again. But the sisters were waiting, so after a moment he forced himself to go on. "Your father shot himself."

That did evoke cries of surprise. It was the middle sister, Tessa, who spoke this time. "I don't believe it," she said. "Papa had far too good an opinion of himself to take his own life. Unless, of course, you mean it was some sort of accident?"

"It was no accident," Mr. James said grimly. "Lord Henley shot himself because he faced ruin. Indeed, he was ruined. Lost every last penny in a card game, including this house, this estate. He had nothing left and decided to take the coward's way out. Forgive me for speaking so bluntly, but he left a letter for me, asking me to inform you three of that fact."

The three sisters sat silent, stunned by the news. Finally, it was Alex who said, "I see. So we are penniless and without a home. Who inherits—? Never mind. It does not matter who inherits the title. It cannot affect us. The more important question, perhaps, is who won the estate and how soon must we leave?"

Mr. James sighed. "As to that, I believe the title

dies with your father. There are, so far as I know, no male heirs to inherit. A Sir Robert Stamford won this estate. Before I left London, I did attempt to discover how soon he would wish to take possession, and he said he had not yet decided. Nor did he seem to know what his plans for this estate might be. I have brought the address of his London town house if you should wish to write to him yourself. Unless, of course, you anticipated such a circumstance and already know where you will go and what you will do?"

Alex rose to her feet and began to pace about the room. "Anticipated such a circumstance? How could we? Though I will allow, in hindsight, that we ought to have done so. Do we know where we will go? No, sir. For as you have so aptly perceived, there is no male left to inherit and no female relatives who would welcome us, either. We shall have to find some course of employment, I suppose. And that will take time. Perhaps you can advise us on how to go about finding work as governesses or companions or housekeepers, sir?"

Mr. James looked from one sister to another to the third and silently cursed the late Lord Henley. How could he have been so irresponsible when he had three daughters at home? And how could he tell them that he had grave doubts of any mother hiring such lovely young women in the first place?

Perhaps it was these thoughts that caused Mr. James to concoct his scheme. Or perhaps it was the fatigue of the journey. But in the end he opened his mouth to say one thing and ended up saying instead, "Let us not be hasty. Perhaps there is an alternative. Housekeeper, you say, Miss Barlow? Perhaps you could write to Sir Robert and offer to stay on as housekeeper here. At least until he chooses to come and take up residence and install a housekeeper more to his liking."

"And how much time will that gain us?" Alex asked, not troubling to hide the bitterness in her voice.

"Perhaps more than you think," Mr. James answered slowly. "Sir Robert has another estate. One close to London that he likes very much. I understand that he has more than once been heard to say he would never bury himself in the countryside when there is so much amusement to be had in London. He is, you see, something of a rake."

"But then won't he wish to sell this place?" Tessa asked with pardonable anxiety.

Mr. James coughed. "Perhaps. But it would take some time to find a buyer. And meanwhile I've no doubt he would be grateful for someone to hold house for him here and keep it maintained until he does find such a buyer. And as I said, that could take some time, with the state of disrepair here and such."

Mr. James eyed Miss Barlow in a meaningful way, and after a startled moment, she nodded her understanding. "Of course," she said slowly. "And what a pity it is the chimneys smoke and the dust lies so thick everywhere and such. But is it fair to play such a trick on this Sir Robert Stamford? Perhaps he needs the funds the sale of this estate would bring?"

"Sir Robert Stamford," Mr. James said, biting off each word, "has more than sufficient funds for his needs, I assure you. That is why I find it particularly reprehensible that he could win this estate from your father when he very well must have known how deep in his cups your father was. He is a reckless young man with no regard for anyone save himself, and most of London would be happy to see him receive the setdown he deserves!"

Alex paced across the room and back again once more before she answered. Guilt warred with need in her breast. The look of fear in her sisters' eyes, however, was what, in the end, decided her.

"Very well," she said. "I shall write to Sir Robert. I daresay he will be very glad to have someone look after this place in his absence."

*　　*　　*

It was less than a week later that Sir Robert Stamford stared at the letter in his hand. What the devil was the meaning of this? he wondered. Lord Henley's daughter wished to stay on as housekeeper on the estate? Stamford vaguely recalled that Henley's solicitor had mentioned something about a daughter, or perhaps more than one. But only to ask how soon he would expect them to leave the estate. This was something altogether different!

For a moment fury possessed the young man accounted one of the *ton*'s most heartless as well as newest members. But it was a fury directed at the late Lord Henley, not at the poor girl who had written this letter. Why the devil had the old fool wagered his entire estate, without even setting aside a small portion for his daughter, and then gone home and put a bullet through his head? Stamford had tried to deal the cards so Henley would win, but it had been impossible. They had taken turns, and the cards had fallen so badly for Henley that Sir Robert had not been able to lose, not even on purpose. And this was the appalling result.

Stamford despised the man, not least for the way he had upset all their plans. But he felt only pity for Henley's daughter. He had a very good notion of just how poor her prospects must be. He wondered if there might be some way to turn that to his advantage. Particularly as he still had to find out about those missing children. Could Henley have been involved? Could it have been one more scheme to try to raise the blunt he needed for the life he desired?

Sir Robert would still need to visit Henley's estate to find out. He could pretend he meant to sell the estate and was making an inspection of the place. But not just yet. He would give her a little more time to mourn first.

He sat down at his writing desk and composed a short but civil letter.

My Dear Miss Barlow,

I should indeed be grateful if you would stay on as housekeeper for a time. I think it unlikely that I shall visit there any time soon and will be grateful to know the house is being looked after properly.

Respectfully,
Sir Robert Stamford

Sir Robert sealed the letter and grimaced. A sour-faced spinster, no doubt, with an abominable temperament, and entirely lacking in looks. How could it be otherwise, with a father like Lord Henley? The man was appallingly ill-favored in his countenance, with a temper to match. How different could the daughter be? Still, even such a creature did not deserve to be cast entirely out of the only home she had likely ever known. And when he came to visit, he would find her knowledge of the neighboring area invaluable.

With that last thought, Stamford set out the letter for a footman to post and dismissed the poor woman from his mind. Particularly as, just at that moment, his dearest friend was shown into the parlor.

"Well, Stamford? Ready for an evening at Almack's?" Lord Ransley demanded.

Robert glared at him. "I do not see," he said through gritted teeth, "why you must drag me there!"

But Lord Ransley only laughed. "You know very well that Lady Ransley insists I go, and if I must go, so shall you. And you know it is her dearest wish to see you wed. Especially since you are in Prinny's black books at the moment. I told you it was a mistake to dangle after his mistress!"

"I was not dangling after his mistress!" Stamford all but shouted. "I was only being polite to the poor creature."

"Yes, well, polite enough so that all she could talk of that evening, apparently, was the delightful Sir Robert Stamford. Prinny was not amused, and if you want to keep your title and your fortune and perhaps even your head, my lady and I had better do our best to see you wed. Or at least looking to be wed. I have it on the best authority that only weekly visits to Almack's and your paying court to the young ladies of the *ton* can possibly keep you from immediate danger of Prinny's wrath!"

Stamford pretended to grumble, but he called for his cloak and followed Lord Ransley out to the waiting carriage where Lady Ransley greeted him with every expression of delight. Stamford smiled in return. And, despite his distaste for the evening ahead, Stamford's smile was genuine.

He liked Lady Ransley. She was one of the few women with any sense. She was not afraid of him, nor did she remind him with veiled barbs of his origins. Besides, if the plan he and Thornsby had devised were to work, he must be seen to be trying to avoid Prinny's wrath. That way, when Prinny, at their behest, banished him entirely from London, no one would think to question that Stamford would go.

Chapter 2

Alex held the laundry list in her hand and went over it yet again. How could so many sheets be used in such a short time? The answer was all too easy and could be found in the cluster of children running wild in the hallways. How had she come to have so many in her care?

The children did not belong here, of course, but what was Alex to do with them? Turn them out? Where would they go? What would they do? If only Margaret did not find so many of them in need of homes! Alex had already imposed upon every family in the village who might be willing to take in a child.

But one did not say no to a woman whose healing potions had pulled more than one estate resident through a nasty bout of illness of one sort or another. Besides, Alex had seen herself the bruises or scars many of the children bore and heard their stories of brutal apprenticeships or abandonment by parents who should have loved them. And how could she turn away the four brothers and sisters whose home had burned down around their heads, killing their parents? She had held more than one child in the middle of the night when terror caused them to cry out in their sleep. No, she could not look at the haunted eyes of these children and tell them they had no refuge here.

It could not last forever. She knew that only too well. One of these days Sir Robert Stamford would find a buyer for this place, despite her best efforts to discourage everyone who came looking. But for now, so long as she had a home, so did these children.

And it wasn't as if she were stealing from Sir Robert by keeping them here and using the estate funds to support them. They were useful, they truly were. Or would have been, if Alex had had the heart to put them to work. But one day they would be stout workers for whomever owned the estate, she told herself. Besides, she simply could not turn them away.

From one room she could hear her sister Tessa's voice telling the younger ones a story she had made up. From another she could hear Lisbeth teaching the older ones their letters. They were both so good with the children! And the children were happy here.

Alex did not like to deceive Sir Robert Stamford, but surely the welfare of these children was far more important than the comfort of a heartless rake, as Mr. James had called him. And Mr. James had assured her that Sir Robert could not possibly need the funds that the sale of this estate would bring him. So, despite her uneasy conscience, Alex meant to go on, as she had begun, taking care of the children, for as long as it was possible to do so.

Sir Robert Stamford stared at the house that loomed before him. It had a singularly unprepossessing facade, and he began, for the first time, to understand why none of the men who had expressed interest in the estate had followed through with an offer to purchase it. He certainly would not have done so if he were in their shoes. He, however, had no choice. He had to come and stay here for as long as it took to uncover what was happening with those missing children.

Stamford sighed. He could not very well return to London any time soon even if he did resolve the mystery. Prinny had seen to that. He had embellished upon the request made to him by Thornsby. A simple request it had been, too. Simply to express disapproval of Stamford and tell him to leave London for a while. There had been no need to add the proviso that Stamford was to marry before he returned.

While he was here, he was going to have to think of a way out of his dilemma. Other than marriage, of course. And it couldn't simply be that Prinny retracted his decree. Otherwise there would be those who began to wonder what was going on. And Stamford and Thornsby couldn't afford to have that happen. Well, at least it was a good thing it was only a sham! Otherwise, if Prinny's disapproval had been real, Stamford would have stood to lose all that he had worked so hard to achieve. And the penniless child he once had been shivered at the thought.

Still, he really wished it was a more prepossessing house! The coachman drew to a halt in the courtyard, and Stamford promptly jumped down from his traveling coach, not bothering with the steps. A curricle, driven by himself, would have been more to his taste, but there was no knowing whether or not he would be obliged to carry any passengers away from here in the relative anonymity of a closed carriage.

"Take it around to the stables," he told the coachman, as one of the footmen hurried to unload his luggage and take it to the top of the steps. "I don't doubt, from the looks of things, that you will have to see to the horses yourself."

The coachman merely gave Stamford a curt nod of assent. Sir Robert hastened to mount the steps to the house, for there was a cold wind blowing despite it being late spring. And when the door was opened by a lugubrious fellow who demanded rather curtly to know what he meant by hammering so hard, Stamford felt it put the final seal on his discontent.

Still, he drew himself to his full height and said, with cool self-possession, "I am Sir Robert Stamford, owner of this place. You will please have the housekeeper, Miss Barlow, I believe, see that a room is made ready for me and my luggage, which you see here, taken up to it for me. Then I wish her to meet me in the library. Meanwhile, you will also direct your cook to prepare a light meal and bring it to me there along with a good bottle of wine."

The man looked taken aback, as well he might. He also looked as if he might argue. But in the end he merely stiffened and said, "Very good, sir. This way."

He showed Stamford to the library, then bowed and added, "Here you are, sir. I am, by the way, Potter. Is there anything else?"

Stamford flushed at this reminder that he had not even bothered to ask the name of the person who, by his manner, probably ranked highest on his staff. Perhaps that was what made his voice sound gruff as he replied, "No, Potter, that will do. Thank you."

The old retainer bowed and left the library, his back stiff with pride. Stamford sighed. He hadn't meant to hurt the fellow's feelings. It was just that even now he hadn't entirely gotten used to how one was supposed to treat servants. Especially not the sort who had been with a family for years and now had to deal with him.

He had to focus on something else. Stamford looked around and took in the way this room had been kept neat and tidy even though the odds were that no one ever used it anymore. If this was the level of housekeeping here, his spirits were much improved, and he had hopes that his stay would not be entirely unpleasant.

In the hallway, it was one of the children, a girl who often crept down to the kitchen to sit with Cook, who came running to find Alex.

"Miss Barlow! Miss Barlow! The new owner be here! The new owner be here!"

Alex dropped the stack of pillowcases she was holding and promptly knelt to pick them up, her thoughts in a whirl. "What do you mean, Mary?"

"Mr. Potter, he come into the kitchen. Said Sir Robert Stamford was in the library, wanting a meal and wine and wanting you to prepare him a room. Then you was to go down and speak to him in the library."

Alex leaned against the nearest wall. The day she had always dreaded was here! But she couldn't give way to fear, not when Mary was looking at her with such wide, frightened eyes.

"Are we all going to be turned out?" the girl whispered.

Alex straightened her shoulders. "Not if I have anything to say about it," she replied. "Come, we must find my sisters and warn them. And then I've a room to prepare for Sir Robert Stamford."

Anyone who knew Miss Barlow well would have understood the meaning of the gleam in her eyes and the half smile on her lips. Anyone who knew her well would have watched with fascinated anticipation for what was undoubtedly about to ensue. But Sir Robert Stamford had no such reason to worry. He only knew, when she entered the library some time later, just as he was finishing the meal Potter had brought him, that Miss Barlow was nothing like what he had expected.

She had made an effort to appear older than she was. Well, she was in mourning for her father. That no doubt accounted for the unrelieved black of her gown, which looked as if it had been let out more than once and did not in the least flatter her. But his fingers itched to pull her blond hair out of the bun she had twisted it into at the back of her neck and pull the horrible lace cap from the top of her head. And why the devil was she staring at him and clutching the locket at her throat as though she were seeing a ghost?

He did not realize he had spoken out loud until she said in withering accents, "I am merely surprised to see you, Sir Robert, that is all. And curious to see what sort of man wins an estate from another. As for my appearance, I do not believe that it is, or need be, your concern. In any event, I thought it best to dress in a way that reminded me I am merely the house-keeper here, no longer the pampered daughter."

Diverted, he asked, "Were you ever the pampered daughter? Somehow I cannot see Lord Henley pampering anyone other than himself."

She was silent so long he thought he had offended her irrevocably and that she did not mean to answer. But when it came, her voice was soft and low and held only longing.

"There was a time I was. Before my mother died. Long ago. Much too long ago." Then she looked at him, really looked at him, and her eyes narrowed. The biting accents came back into her voice as she said, "I cannot see what any of this signifies to you."

He waved a hand carelessly. "Say that I am eccentric. Say that I like to know about the people in my employ. Which reminds me, I have not been sending you wages for your post here as my housekeeper. Indeed, I do not think we ever discussed how much they should be. Will three hundred guineas per year do?"

"T-t-three hundred?"

Stamford rather enjoyed watching her gasp of disbelief. But she recovered quickly, more quickly than he would have expected.

She drew herself up, sniffed, and said with a hint of disdain in her voice, "I believe it will suffice."

He could not resist teasing her. "If you are dissatisfied and would prefer to quit my employ . . ."

"No!"

The answer came with gratifying speed. And then she colored up a fiery red. Robert could not have said why he enjoyed taunting her. Indeed, under most circumstances he would have found it contemptible. But he found himself wanting to know all about this woman and seeing her unguarded reactions to his words was a promising start. It was only, he told himself, because he might need her help and he needed to know what sort of woman she might be.

But he'd given her too much time with his wandering thoughts. She was once again self-possessed, and she began to tell him all about his new estate.

"I have put you in the master bedroom. The chimney smokes, but then they all do. The east wing is in sad need of repairs, and I suggest you avoid it altogether until someone can show you the safe and unsafe places to go. The west wing, where your bedroom is, is in somewhat better shape. Your apartment, which was my father's, is the only one, however, that has seen any money spent on it in more than a decade. The main hall is, as you may have noticed, a splendid example of former glory now in decline. The gardens are in somewhat better shape, but only if one prefers the wild and natural effect. Some would say they would be better for a good pruning."

She rattled it all off, Stamford thought, as though giving a tour of the place. Was that what potential buyers had heard when they came to look at the place? Good God, no wonder it had not sold! Granted, it would not have suited his plans if anyone had actually decided to purchase the place but still, it galled him to know the chit had had a hand in the absence of any offers.

Still, perhaps she merely spoke the literal truth. From what he had seen so far, that could well be the case. Lord Henley had patently not wanted to waste his blunt on repairs or upkeep of a home he could not have visited above twice a year and for very brief stretches at that.

Which meant his daughter was no doubt accustomed to run wild and do as she wished. Well, he could not blame her for not wanting that to change. Unfortunately, in this life, one almost always had to face change. Sometimes it was good and sometimes, as it was today for both him and for her, it was something one had to endure.

"I like being here no more than you like having me," he told her bluntly as he rose to his feet. "But as I am here, we shall both have to make do. You may as well become accustomed to my tongue, and I shall endeavor to become accustomed to yours, Miss Barlow. At least you give me hope that I shall not be bored while I am here. Now, suppose you show me the way to this master bedroom, as you call it. I have traveled hard and fast and not gotten much sleep. I think I could do with a nap."

She gaped at him as though he were wanting in wits. Or as if she were. Or perhaps it was merely his height, for Stamford was a tall man. Not that she was a petite creature herself. There could not be many men she had had to look up to, as she had to do with him.

Abruptly, she recollected herself, however, and gave a quick nod. "Very well. This way, Sir Robert. I trust that by now your valet has been shown upstairs and will have your things unpacked."

"I did not bring my valet," Stamford countered, matching her stride for stride, step for step as they started up the main stairs. "I am accustomed," he added when she turned an astonished gaze on him, "to look after myself."

"Yes, sir. I see. Well, this is the west wing over here. Your doorway is at the far end. That allowed the apartment to be of extraordinary size. It is considered handsome."

"So long as one does not mind the chimney smoking," Stamford could not resist adding.

She looked at him as though trying to decide if he was roasting her. Her voice held reproof as she said, "It does not always smoke, only most of the time. No doubt that is something you can arrange to have repaired if you choose to spend your blunt that way. Though since I presume you do not mean to stay longer than needed to inspect this place, you may not wish to bother."

He paused, forcing her to pause as well. "Why do you presume I do not mean to stay long?" he asked, his eyes probing hers, his instincts suddenly on alert, though he could not have said why.

She blinked at him. "B-because you like London. I am told you are accounted a notable gambler and like to be surrounded by the delights of the city. Why would you want to stay here? Particularly as your own estate is much more handsomely appointed."

His eyes narrowed. "You seem remarkably well informed about my affairs," he said, grasping her arm.

She stiffened at the accusation implicit in his words. "My father's solicitor, when he came to inform us of the change in our circumstances," she said, biting off each word, "told us everything he knew about you."

"Us?" Stamford all but pounced on the word.

For a moment he thought she would not answer. With no attempt to hide her anger, she pulled her arm free from his grasp. She held herself with a dignity far above the circumstances to which she now found herself reduced. He felt himself once again the young boy chased out of places others felt he didn't belong, and he had to fight the urge to run away. This was his house now, he reminded himself. She was the one who had to answer to him.

"Us," she repeated. "My two sisters and myself."

"And where are your sisters?" Stamford demanded. "Why are you not living with one of them?"

"Because, Sir Robert, none of us is married, and we are all living here."

Chapter 3

Sir Robert stared at Miss Barlow, thunderstruck. She had not only had the audacity to propose herself as housekeeper, which he had generously agreed to, but kept her sisters on here as well? And he supposed, he thought wryly, that he would figure as the villain of the piece in the eyes of the *ton* if he threw them all out on their ears as they deserved. It was fortunate that it would serve his purpose very well to have them here awhile longer.

"I suppose your sisters are acting as housemaids, or something of the sort?"

"No."

Just that one word, spoken with disdain. No attempt to apologize, no attempt to explain or justify what she had done. Well, Stamford gave her credit for keeping a cool head under trying circumstances. The question was, what ought he to do now?

"Where *are* your sisters?" he asked.

"You will meet them at dinner," was all she would say.

Then, without giving him a chance to question her further, she went on ahead and threw open a set of double doors. "Here is your chamber, Sir Robert. I shall leave you to your nap, and I shall see you at dinner as well."

Before he could recover his wits sufficiently to think of a reason to stop her, Miss Barlow headed back down the hallway and then ran lightly down the stairs, no doubt to find her sisters and warn them.

Well, let her, he told himself. She had said he would meet them at dinner. Very well, then at dinner it would be. But mark me well, he thought, one way or another, there would be a full accounting of their extraordinary behavior. Meanwhile, while she thought he was napping, Stamford intended to slip down the back stairs and outside and look around the land he now so unexpectedly owned.

Robert intended to see what there was to see before anyone had a chance to hide anything more from him. He didn't bother to stop and ask himself why they should do so, or try to answer. It was too ingrained a part of him that in their shoes, if someone had won the land he lived on, he would have wanted to protect whatever he could. And besides, there was the matter of the children. The faster he could find out whether they were here and, if so, what was going on, the sooner he could leave.

Alex was trembling when she found her sisters. They were, as she expected, with the children. And they were, unexpectedly, quiet.

"Mary warned us," Tessa explained. "Is Sir Robert Stamford really here? How long does he mean to stay? Does he know about us?"

"Yes, he really is here," Alex agreed. "He knows about the three of us, but not about the children. And I don't mean for him to find out. I don't know how long he means to stay. I tried to ask him but somehow he never answered."

"What are we going to do?" Lisbeth asked, practical as ever. "Does he mean to send us away?"

Alex hesitated. "I don't know. Perhaps he will tell us at dinner. He expects to meet both of you then. We shall have to be careful that none of us slips and mentions the children. That was my mistake, you see, not watching my tongue carefully enough. Otherwise even your existence would be a secret to him too."

Tessa shook her head and said, "It is just as well

that he knows about Lisbeth and me. If he means to
stay here any time at all and goes to the village or
even to church, he would hear us mentioned. Better
he should find out from you that we are here. But the
children, yes, we must be careful to hide their existence. Even if he is willing to let Lisbeth and me stay,
somehow I think he would draw the line at having
them here as well."

The three sisters nodded as one, and Alex found
her hand creeping to the locket at her throat. She had
not told her sisters the oddest thing of all, that Sir
Robert Stamford looked exactly like the face she had
seen in the locket the day Margaret had given it to
her.

It must be my imagination, she told herself firmly.
Both thinking she saw a face that day and now thinking it resembled Sir Robert's. And even if it did, he
was far too handsome, with his dark hair and deep
brown eyes, and far too wealthy to ever look twice at
her. She was only his housekeeper, after all, and not
one that he was very happy with! She must be sensible, Alex told herself firmly. Her sisters and the children needed her to keep her wits about her.

Oddly enough, clutching the locket gave her comfort and steadied her emotions. But perhaps that
wasn't so odd, given that it was one of the few things
she had left from her mother. If only Papa had not
insisted on ridding the house of all reminders of her
after she had died! Was it Alex's imagination that the
locket warmed under her grasp? Or that she seemed
to hear her mother's voice whispering that all would
be well?

Alex shook her head impatiently. There was no use,
nor time to spare, either, to dwell on the past. She
and her sisters must decide what to do about the children. She looked at them thoughtfully.

"If any of you," she said to the children slowly,
"should encounter a stranger in or near the house,
you must assume it is Sir Robert Stamford, and you

must pretend to be one of the servants. Polish the furniture or pretend to be fixing something. Anything so he does not guess the truth! Once he is gone, then we can go back to how things were."

All of the children nodded. There were roughly a dozen now. "You'll need to keep Sara and Peter out of sight," Lisbeth told the older ones.

"And keep them from crying at night," Tessa added. "Though if he hears them, we shall simply say that the east wing is haunted. You did tell him it was not safe to explore, didn't you?" she asked her sister anxiously.

"Yes, but I fear it only piqued his curiosity," Alex replied bitterly.

"The first time he puts his foot through a rotten floorboard, of which there are far too many, he will believe you," Lisbeth said with grim satisfaction.

"I hope you may be right. Meanwhile, I'd best go down to the kitchen and warn Potter and Cook and the others not to let on about the children either," Alex said. "Fortunately, he did not bring a valet, so that is one less pair of eyes to worry about. And I presume his coachman and footmen will spend most of their time down by the stables. Perhaps you, Harry," she said, picking out the oldest boy, who liked horses, "could pretend to be working in the stables and keep an eye on all of them?"

Harry grinned. "I'll go down there right now. I'd like that, I would. And don't you worry none, I won't let 'em see nuffing they shouldn't."

The boy was gone before Alex could ask what he meant. She only hoped he didn't take his promise too seriously. The last thing they needed was an overzealous attempt to protect them all. Still, it was good to know someone would be keeping an eye on Stamford's men. Experience had taught Alex that servants often discovered family secrets that guests would otherwise never know.

"Go on down to the kitchen," Tessa urged her,

breaking into Alex's thoughts. "We will arrange things with the children, perhaps move them farther back into the east wing so that Sir Robert is less likely to see or hear them."

Alex nodded. Her sister was right. There was no time to be lost. Sir Robert had said he meant to take a nap, but who knew how long that would last? Fear made her move swiftly down the servants' stairs and to the kitchens where Cook and Potter were happily engaged in ripping their new master's character to shreds.

"Didn't even ask me name," Potter said with a sniff.

"Nor think to send on word ahead he were coming," Cook added for good measure. "Didn't care what trouble he caused, showing up unannounced like. Never touched half the food on the tray you took to him in the library. I suppose he'll say my cooking's not good enough for the likes of him."

"I'm sure that's not it," Alex said in soothing tones as she came toward the pair. "I'm afraid I interrupted him and he forgot to finish it."

Cook sniffed. "Like as not it were just an excuse. I've heard about his sort. Just like your father, I'll be bound. None of the sauces was fancy enough for him, neither. If he'd been able to find another cook willing to abide here or if he'd settled here longer than a week or two at a time, I'd have had my walking papers I'll be bound."

"Speaking of settled here," Potter said diffidently, "how long does Sir Robert mean to stay, Miss Barlow?"

Alex shrugged. "I don't know. Not very long, I hope. But he did not tell me."

"Well, it had best be a short stay or he's bound to find out about them brats of yours," Cook warned.

Unconsciously, Alex hunched her shoulders. "I hope not," she said. "We mean to hide them as best we can. We managed to do it while Papa was alive and came home, so surely we can do it now, with Sir Robert."

"Your papa was half drunk most of the time he were home. And you didn't have so many children here then," Cook told her roundly.

"We must still try," she said resolutely.

"What will you do if Sir Robert does find out?" Potter asked.

Alex looked at her, a bleak expression in her eyes. "I don't know," she admitted. "But no matter what, I will not let him hurt my children or send them away!"

"Oh, and you've the means to stop him, I suppose!" Cook said with a derisive snort.

Alex's voice was grim as she replied, "One way or another, I'd find the means. I'll not let him take my children away from me!"

In the hallway, one of the footmen, Dunford, listened with avid ears. So the lady had children and was hiding them, was she? He'd bet Sir Robert would give a great deal to know about that. Aye, and not like it either that she was housing them at his expense.

Not that he meant to tell Stamford. The man might pay well, but he wasn't what you could call a warm or kindly man. Not one to ask or care about the troubles or wishes any of his servants might have.

By rights he ought to still be in London, Dunford thought. That was what he'd been hired for and thinking himself very lucky and well suited to be there. But now he was here, a long way from where he wanted or expected to be. But try to tell that to Sir Robert. No, only his convenience mattered. To be sure he paid well for such service, but there were times when other things mattered more than the money, and Dunford wished he'd had the courage to say so before they set out.

Well, he was here now, and there was nothing to be done about that. And Dunford would keep his eyes and ears open, he would. But that didn't mean he'd tell Sir Robert everything he learned. There might be even more profit in keeping a still tongue in his head, and until he knew which way the wind blew, he wasn't about to say a word.

He listened for a while longer, but the lady was talking only about what might be suitable for Sir Robert's dinner. Clearly she was torn between wanting to give him a disgust of the place and wanting him to value her services as a housekeeper. When it became clear he would hear nothing more that was useful, at least not to him, Dunford silently crept out of the house. Had he known Sir Robert was watching, he might not have congratulated himself so thoroughly on his cleverness. But since he had no notion, Dunford was quite pleased with the results of his charade.

Sir Robert, meanwhile, observed his footman with a grim expression. He could guess precisely what the fellow was about, and while he did not blame him, he wondered if Dunford would confide in him whatever it was he had overheard.

Somehow Stamford didn't think so. He didn't know how or why, he only knew that he had never acquired the knack that his friend Lord Ransley seemed to have had since birth, of commanding not only the loyalty but also the affection of his servants. It was a talent Stamford envied. And yet it was one he could not see how he could possibly acquire. So he resigned himself to his footman perhaps knowing more about what was going on here than he did himself. Still, he filed away the information for later. If he needed an ally in finding out about the children, a man as curious as Dunford might prove very useful.

Sir Robert sighed. It was lovely hereabouts—rolling hillsides, lots of trees, meadows full of flowers. It was, he thought, a peaceful place. Unlike his own estate, near London, one didn't hear or expect to hear the constant sound of carriages bringing guests wishing to take advantage of his hospitality. There was a sense of isolation he found very appealing.

But it was foolish to think this way. He had a job to do, and once it was done he would be returning to London. If, that is, he could also figure out what to do about Prinny's absurd command to marry.

Perhaps if the job took long enough, they could give out that Prinny had remembered why he had valued his services so highly in the first place that he arranged for his rise to the title of Sir Robert. And that he had sent for Stamford to return.

With a sigh, Stamford looked up at the east wing. Was it really in as horrible shape as Miss Barlow had said, he wondered. Even as he was studying the stone facade of the wing, a face appeared at one of the windows. The face was small and pale and looked like that of a child.

But that was impossible, Robert told himself. There could be, should be no children at the house. Even if Henley had been involved in whatever was happening with the children, he would surely not have been so foolish as to house them here! The man was the highest of sticklers when it came to his own consequence, and he would never have agreed to house the abducted children in his own home. No, it must have been one of the maids.

But it had certainly looked like the face of a boy. And something in the child's expression had reminded him of himself. That was what felt so strange, Robert told himself, that was why he suddenly felt a chill. Still, perhaps he would ask Miss Barlow a few more pertinent questions about the east wing when he saw her at dinner.

Miss Barlow did not seem to be the sort of woman who could lie well. Stamford would know if she tried, and the likeliest possibility, in any event, was that she would set his unsettled emotions to rest by telling him whose face he had seen. And if, by chance, she was foolish enough to be hiding children here, he would soon know that as well.

With such firm intention, Sir Robert began to stroll

back toward the house. Time enough tomorrow to ride out to see his land. Assuming, of course, that Lord Henley had left even one reliable horse in the stable. The head groom had been remarkably reluctant to tell him anything. That, he thought bitterly, was what came of dealing with old family retainers. It was all but impossible to persuade them that their loyalty now belonged to someone else, no matter what legal papers one might hold.

Chapter 4

Alex, Tessa, and Lisbeth wore their best dark-colored gowns to dinner. Best, of course, was a relative term. None of the gowns was new, and all three had been mended often. But they were the best these three women owned that were even remotely appropriate for mourning.

"It is very fortunate," Alex told her sisters, "that none of us looks our best in these depressing colors."

"Why?" Lisbeth asked with wide-eyed innocence.

"Don't you remember?" Tessa demanded impatiently. "Mr. James told us that Sir Robert Stamford is a notorious rake! You must have met at least one rake when you had your Season. Surely you understand that we don't precisely want him to think us attractive."

Lisbeth did remember; she did understand. "Oh. Yes, of course."

"Never mind that," Alex said impatiently. "We must remember to mind our tongues. Ask him about himself instead of talking about ourselves or Henley Hall. That ought to be easy enough. Men always like to talk about themselves."

The other two sisters nodded. That had certainly been their experience as well. With one last glance in the looking glass, all three sisters left the bedroom and headed for the stairs.

Sir Robert Stamford was already in the drawing room, waiting for them. It was easy to see that he was from London, for he was dressed in clothes that could not have been made anywhere else. His coat was cut too neatly, his boots had too high a polish, and his neck cloth was tied in far too intricate a fashion for anyone, even the three sisters, to ever mistake him for a provincial fellow.

He lifted his quizzing glass when they entered the room and studied the sisters from head to toe and back again. The silence stretched on so long that Alexandra's temper began to rise and with it her color. Apparently, Sir Robert noticed, for abruptly he dropped his quizzing glass and came forward to greet her.

"Will you not introduce your sisters to me, Miss Barlow?" he asked politely.

"This is my sister, Elizabeth, and my other sister, Theresa," Alex said with less than a gracious manner.

He bowed. "Charmed, ladies, even if you are a trifle surprising."

That left them all with a sense of confusion. Whatever did he mean? He did not leave them in doubt for long.

"Why are you not in London? All of you?" he asked.

"Our father left us penniless. He lost everything to you in a game of cards," Alex pointed out. "Or perhaps you were so far gone in your cups that you do not remember."

He chose to be amused. "I remember," he said, twirling his quizzing glass. "But I meant, why did your father not bring you out? Surely, he could have made advantageous matches for all three of you, even if he did have to scrimp on the dowries."

It was Lisbeth who answered. She tilted up her chin. "We did each have a Season."

Stamford frowned. "You cannot tell me you did not take! I should not believe it of any of you."

"Oh, we took," Tessa now replied. "We each had our share of offers. And we turned them all down."

Had he asked why, they might have refused to tell

him. But he did not. He merely stared at them, one eyebrow raised in patent disbelief. Lisbeth all but stamped her foot as she said, "It is true! We each could have married, but we chose not to."

"Why?"

Again, perhaps it was the calm way he asked the question that prompted Alex to answer. Later, she could not think what else it could have been that would have prompted her to speak of something so personal to this stranger.

"Because we saw our father and how he was with our mother—the power he had over every aspect of her life. And none of us wanted that for ourselves. To be under the thumb of a man, with no rights of our own, would have been intolerable. So would having to watch as he took mistress after mistress while our own hearts broke."

"You need not have married for love," Stamford pointed out. "And then you wouldn't have cared if your husbands took mistresses."

"We would not marry for anything else," Tessa answered with quiet dignity, "no matter how hard Papa pressed us to do so."

Stamford shook his head. It was the most extraordinary conversation he could remember in some time. "You preferred to be spinsters? Ape leaders?" he demanded.

"Yes!"

They spoke as one, and he could not mistake their fervor. He shrugged. "Well, it is your own affair, I suppose. Though I cannot see what you will do now that you are left penniless. Anything, I should have thought, would have been preferable to that."

It was Lisbeth who said quietly, "That is because you do not know the men that Papa chose for us."

He was spared the need to answer that because Potter came to announce that dinner was ready to be served. Stamford escorted Miss Barlow in to the dining room. She sat at his right, the second eldest at his left, and the third on the other side of Miss Barlow. From their expressions it was going, Robert resigned himself with a sigh, to be a very long, very dreary meal.

But he was mistaken. They tried to prompt him to talk about himself. Amused, he refused and wondered if they would then resort to silence. But they did not. As much as they might have wanted to snub him, they could not resist talking with one another, and in listening Stamford learned a great deal about the estate he had inherited. He learned the names of some of his tenants and he learned about some of their problems. It was most distressing to realize that instead of a windfall, he'd inherited an estate neglected far too long by its owner. And yet, he thought, he ought to have guessed how it would be, for he'd often enough thought that Lord Henley was not a man to spend his blunt on anyone's comfort save his own.

Abruptly, he broke into their conversation and said, "Tomorrow, Miss Barlow, I should like you to take me to meet these people."

There was a stunned silence at his words. It was the youngest sister who asked bluntly, "Why?"

Sir Robert Stamford favored Miss Elizabeth Barlow with the stare many had called terrifying. She was not in the least daunted.

"Why do you want to see these people?" she repeated. "Do you mean to turn them off the land for complaining?"

Stamford was too astonished to reply. It was Alex who explained gently, "That is what our father might have done. You, I am persuaded, would not be nearly so cruel."

"And why should you believe that?" he could not resist asking. "How do you know I am not as cruel as your father would have been?"

She merely regarded him placidly over her trifle and smiled. "Because while Father, in your shoes, might have allowed me to stay on here as housekeeper, he would never have offered to pay me wages for doing so."

Stamford flushed. He was not accustomed to being summed up so accurately by anyone, much less someone he had just met. It was patent, however, that her words were met with approval by her sisters, who now smiled at him with far greater warmth than before. He could not, he found, destroy their approval with a lie, and it would have been a lie to say that he would turn out the tenants.

"Very well, you are correct," he said curtly. "But I do not relish, nor does any man, Miss Barlow, having his affairs bandied about in such a way."

"Of course. Forgive me, Sir Robert," she said with deceptive meekness.

It was a meekness he did not trust, did not want to trust, he realized. He preferred the spirit she had shown him heretofore and was annoyed to discover such a preference. He did not wish to like Miss Barlow, spirited or otherwise. She was merely a nuisance, to be tolerated for so long as he stayed. Or a possible ally in finding out about the children. He did not wish to become intrigued by the contradictions in her nature.

"Tell me," he said with as careless an air as he could manage, "are there many children hereabouts?"

All three sisters stared at him. Miss Barlow's eyes narrowed with suspicion. "Why should you care about that?" she demanded.

He shrugged. "I don't, particularly. I was simply making conversation. You are ladies, therefore I assumed the subject would interest you."

It was the best answer he could think of, and he knew it to be a very weak one. Miss Barlow continued to regard him with a frown even as her sisters made an effort to distract him. They pelted Stamford with questions about London.

Perhaps the three sisters had visited the city for a Season each, but it was evident their father had had but one thought in mind in bringing them there and permitted them nothing that did not directly involve the pursuit of a husband. There were many, many places they had not seen, many things about which they were curious, and so many things they wished him to explain.

Stamford did his best, but there was no doubt he was feeling harried. When Potter set the bottle of brandy on the table before him, it was with great relief that Robert greeted this signal to the ladies to retire to the drawing room. He all but mopped his brow as he rose to watch them leave the room.

Once they were gone, he exchanged a smile with Potter, who moved forward to pour him a glass of the brandy. Then, as though he had been with Stamford for years, rather than Lord Henley's servant, Potter said with a marked degree of sympathy, "They are lonely, sir. High-spirited and lonely—an unfortunate combination. But they will be better now that you are here."

Before Stamford could ask the fellow what he meant by such an impertinent statement, Potter removed himself and the footmen from the room, leaving him alone with his thoughts. Unfortunately, for perhaps the first time in his life, Robert found that he did not wish to be alone with his thoughts.

In spite of their annoying questions, he found he missed the company of the three Barlow sisters. He missed their laughter, their chatter, their very enthusiasm, for it was something he himself had lost a long time ago. And he still needed to find out about the children!

So despite his better judgment, despite the existence of as fine a brandy as any man could want, Sir Robert Stamford downed his drink in one swallow and rose to follow the ladies. He might have had some trouble finding them except that the sound of voices drew him inexorably down the right hallway.

The door to the drawing room stood open part way,

and he paused, watching and listening to a scene of domestic tranquillity such as he had never known. He had never seen his mother or sisters bent over a pile of mending, or sitting at a finely crafted writing desk, or sitting at the pianoforte, playing a simple ballad.

He would have turned away then and sought the cool air outdoors, but he must have made a sound, for suddenly the ladies looked up and saw him standing there. Immediately, they called out, inviting him to come and join them. It was, Stamford discovered, an invitation he could not bring himself to decline.

"Do you know this song?" Lisbeth asked, playing the notes again. "I am looking for someone to sing it with me."

Stamford shook his head, not trusting himself to speak. How could he explain that he had never had a chance to learn such things? Or that he didn't wish to see the eldest whisk away her mending, as though it were something to be ashamed of? Or that he wanted to ask the middle sister what it was she was writing?

He was who and what he was, and he had sworn long ago never to feel ashamed, but promises don't always translate very well to truth. So now he merely took the nearest chair and sank into it. He took refuge in the cool irony that had been his shield in the midst of the *ton*.

"A very pleasant domestic scene. But surely there are servants to do the mending, Miss Barlow?"

"They have quite enough to do as it is," she retorted, defiantly pulling out the mending again and once more setting her needle to work.

"Do you never miss dancing? Or going to parties?" he could not help but ask.

She looked at him, and there was something, perhaps pity, in her eyes as she replied, "Of what use, Sir Robert, would it be for me to miss what I cannot have? I am accustomed to my circumstances, and had dancing"—she stressed the word in such a way that he flushed—"been of such great importance to me, I

must have accepted one of the offers made to me
during my Season so that I could always dance when
I wished."

And that set him neatly in his place! He turned to
the middle sister, and she was regarding him with wry
sympathy. Did none of them realize their precarious
position here? Did none of them care?

The youngest began to play a plaintive melody, and
Stamford recognized it as one that had been popular
a few Seasons before. So perhaps the youngest sister
did have regrets, after all. But he could not ask her,
not after the setdown the eldest had given him. Instead, he turned to the middle sister and asked, "What
are you writing so industriously, Miss Theresa
Barlow?"

She flushed. "N-n-nothing," she stammered.

"A love letter perhaps?" he suggested teasingly.

She seized on the notion with alarming speed. "Yes,
yes. That's it! A love letter!"

Her sisters realized her mistake, but she did not.
Not soon enough, at any rate. Stamford leaned forward. "So it is not a love letter," he said with a frown.
"But what else would you be afraid to admit to
writing?"

Miss Theresa Barlow shrank back in her chair, but
the eldest sister was made of stronger mettle. She rose
to her feet and moved to stand between Sir Robert
and her younger sisters.

"That is quite enough," she said. "We are well
aware that we are here on your sufferance, sir, but I
cannot think it kind in you to toy with us this way."

Stamford looked at her, taken aback by the truth
in her words. He did not like the portrait she painted
of him. He was here to find out about missing children, not to cut up the peace of three women who
had no choice but to depend upon his generosity. Now
he was the one who rose to his feet, and he was the
one who flushed with embarrassment. He bowed.

"You are right, of course, Miss Barlow. Therefore,

before I make myself any more odious than I already have, I shall bid you ladies good night and leave you to your amusements. Miss Barlow, I shall see you in the morning. I still wish to ride out to meet these tenants you spoke about at dinner."

Chapter 5

Stamford woke, knowing he'd heard something out of place, but not knowing what it was. Then he heard it again. A child's cry. It was a sound one could not escape when he was growing up, nor mistake for anything else now. He threw off the covers and was halfway to the door before he realized the enormity of what he was thinking.

A child—crying here. Could it really be that someone was hiding the missing children here? In the house? He might easily have believed Lord Henley had been trafficking in children, but the Barlow sisters? Impossible! He stood for some time, listening, but the sound did not come again. The child, if child it was, was silent now. Could he have been mistaken? He did not think so, and yet the alternative seemed even more improbable.

Stamford considered going out into the hallway and looking for the source of the sound. Except that he could not be certain he had not simply been dreaming. Besides, it would not suit his purpose to be caught snooping about. No, he wanted to lull everyone here into thinking him the harmless fellow he had taken such pains to seem to be.

Tomorrow he would ask Miss Barlow about the sound. Even if it was real, there might be a simple explanation. In a household as unconventional as this, it was possible, for example, that a servant might have been given permission to keep her child with her.

So he sought his bed again and was soon asleep. He

never heard the soft footsteps creep past his bedroom door or the soft lullaby sung in the east wing. He never knew that even if he had tried to leave his room, he could not have done so, for the key that was in the lock overnight was removed before he woke in the morning.

"Miss Barlow, you are dressed for riding!" Stamford exclaimed, checking in the doorway of the small breakfast parlor.

Alex looked at him with level eyes. "Of course, Sir Robert. You said you wished to visit the tenants." She paused and took in his own attire. "You are not dressed for riding," she said flatly. "Did I misunderstand?"

She would have sworn he was impatient with himself as he moved forward and took the seat next to hers. "No, you did not," he acknowledged as he poured himself tea. "I simply had not expected you to be ready this early."

"This early?" she echoed with some astonishment. Then her gaze lowered, and she kept it carefully fixed on her plate as she said, "Ah, of course. I should have recollected that you would likely keep London hours. My apologies. I shall change and take care of other things first. Just tell me when you wish to leave and I shall change back again."

She could feel, rather than see, his scowl, and she was hard put not to smile in return. Nor was she surprised when he said a trifle impatiently, "No, no, do not bother. Give me half an hour to dine and then another quarter hour to change and I shall be ready to set out. The earlier the better. We are, after all, in the country, and country hours I shall keep while I am here."

Alex breathed a silent sigh of relief, but she was a trifle premature, for abruptly he asked, "Is there a child in the house."

"A ch-child?"

"Yes, a child. You know, a miniature adult?"

"W-why do you ask, sir?"

"Because I thought I heard one last night," he said, his irritation evident.

Alex forced herself to relax and look at him with a smile. "Oh. The child. Everyone who stays here hears the child. I should, perhaps, have warned you. But I thought your nerves were such that you would not hear the child."

"Well, who the devil's is it?"

She lowered her eyes. "They say," she said in a careless voice, "that it belongs to the third Lady Henley. The one who threw herself from a window just under the eaves and fell to her death. They say the child cries for her. He died, you see, within the month after she did."

"A ghost?"

It was evident he was taken aback by her words. Alex now had to hide the smile that quivered at the corners of her lips. Thank heavens for Tessa's fertile imagination!

"So they say," she told him gravely.

He shook his head. "I don't believe in ghosts."

"Neither do I," Alex said, her voice still grave and perfectly even.

Sir Robert looked at her with narrowed eyes, but she met his gaze firmly. It was, after all, the truth. Tessa had created a legend of a ghost child who cried in the night for his mother, and Alexandra did not believe in ghosts. It was simply applying it to this circumstance that was the prevarication.

But perhaps she betrayed her nervousness by the way she fingered the locket around her neck, for suddenly his eyes fixed on that. And Alex found herself explaining, even though he did not ask.

"It was my mother's. She left it for me in the care of a local wise woman. I have only had it a short time, you see, and so it is very precious to me."

He nodded. "Yes, of course it would be. My pardon for staring. It is just that it is most unusual."

Alex did not trust herself to answer. Fortunately, he asked nothing more, but turned his attention to his food. She tried to eat as well. But she could not swallow food with him beside her, and she could only be grateful for the habit that caused her to rise before almost anyone else in the house. Let her sisters deal with Sir Robert if he was still here when they came downstairs. She would go and speak to Cook until it was time to ride out with Stamford.

She half thought he would protest her desertion. But beyond an amused smile, as if he could see her discomfort, he did and said nothing. He merely nodded when Alex told him that she would meet him by the stables in three quarters of an hour.

Robert grimaced as the horse under him stumbled yet again. "Had your father no better mounts in his stable than these?" he demanded.

Miss Barlow looked at him and smiled wryly. "Oh, yes, there was a time when he had the best stable for miles around. But then he had to sell his horses, one by one. The only mounts left are those that no one could possibly want."

"I see. Is there nothing about this estate to recommend it, then?"

She hesitated, and he could see the shadow in her eyes. For a moment Robert regretted his blunt speaking. But he was not in the best of spirits this morning. He could not help thinking he ought to have investigated the sound last night, after all. If there was a legend of a ghost child crying, then perhaps someone had used it to good purpose to cover the presence of a child in the house. Though why the child would be kept in Henley Hall he still could not imagine!

To be sure, Henley himself might have had the sort of tastes that would lead to his buying stolen children. But he could not imagine such a thing of the three

women now living in the house. It made no sense.
And because he disliked things that made no sense,
Stamford was in a foul mood. And yet, he reminded
himself, Miss Barlow had no easier a time of it than
he did. It must have been a severe shock to her to
have him descend upon the house without warning.
And she ought never to have been put in such a position in the first place!

"I'm sorry," he said gently. "I did not mean to rail
at you. I simply do not understand how your father
could squander his inheritance in such a way."

She smiled, but the shadows were still in her eyes
as she replied, "Nor I. You see only the lack, Sir Robert, as did he. An old house in need of repairs, gardens
in need of care, a stable empty of any desirable
mounts. But I see the countryside, beautiful most of
the time and as fertile as any one could wish for. I
know the people hereabouts, and most of them are
good and gentle souls. This could have been a happy
place, had my father only been content to see it in
such a way, rather than as a resource to cover his
gambling debts."

Robert nodded, wishing he could reach out and
touch her rosy cheeks or tug at one of the curls that
framed her face beneath the green bonnet that
matched her habit. It was the first time he had seen
her in colors since he arrived, and he guessed that had
she had the funds to have a black riding habit made
up, he would not see her in them, even now.

Abruptly he realized she was speaking to him.

". . . the village."

He looked around. It was a paltry place. Small, with
few shops or even homes. Many seemed in need of
repairs. He looked at her, and even before he could
frame the question it was as if she read his mind.
"Father would not spend the money on the village.
Said that if they minded the flaws in their homes they
would find a way to fix them."

"I see."

And he did. A grim feeling settled over him as he imagined the life Lord Henley's daughters must have led as well as Lord Henley's tenants. It was a wonder the man was not universally hated hereabouts. Or perhaps he was. If so, it was a feeling that could easily be transferred over to him if he were not careful to distinguish himself quickly from the previous owner of the estate.

But the people who came out to greet them seemed friendly enough, if a little wary. Well, he was wary too. And alert for any signs of children who did not belong or anyone who might be afraid of strangers nosing about.

Stamford pretended to play the part of a new landowner interested in learning everything there was to know about his land and his tenants. And indeed, so long as he held these lands, they were his responsibility. So Robert listened, looked at the buildings and the problems that were shown him, and promised to see that the most urgent repairs were undertaken promptly. Gradually, it seemed, the villagers warmed to him. It was only when they reached the smithy that there was a problem.

Robert had noticed that the closer they got, the more Miss Barlow seemed to stiffen her spine. He sensed she disliked the man, not from what she said but from what she didn't say. The laughing tone was gone from her voice as she told him about the couple. There was no complaint precisely, merely a lack of the warmth she had shown everyone else.

The smith and his wife came out to greet them, but only briefly. "I be needing to do me work," the smith said and turned his back on them.

The wife, however, timidly offered them some of her cowslip wine. Miss Barlow smiled warmly at the woman, and though she declined the wine, asked after her health with some anxiety, it seemed to Stamford.

Perhaps that was what made him look so closely at the woman. Close enough to see the faint remains of

a bruise at her temple and another at her jawbone.
He guessed they were not the first she had suffered.
She had the air of a woman thoroughly cowed by
her husband.

Instinctively, his hands clenched into fists at his side.
So that was why Miss Barlow disliked the smith! Well,
he disliked the man as well. Robert had no use for
cowards, and only a coward would strike a woman,
particularly a woman so much smaller than himself. It
made him think too much of times he would rather
forget.

Something must have caught Miss Barlow's eye, for
suddenly he felt her hand on his arm. And he realized
she was regarding him with some concern. He shook
both off with some impatience. "Are we ready to go,
Miss Barlow?" he asked coldly. "I believe I have seen
as much as I need to see."

The smith's wife was taken aback and so was Miss
Barlow. She did not argue, however, but kept her silence until they were some distance from the village.

Then she looked at him and said, "My apologies,
Sir Robert. I did not mean to bore you. But it was
you who said you wished to meet your tenants."

He pulled his horse up short, causing her to do the
same. "On the contrary, Miss Barlow, it is I who owe
you an apology. I was neither bored nor upset with
you in any way."

"Then—" She started to ask but cut herself short.
"My accursed curiosity! It is not my affair, after all."

Stamford drew in a deep breath. "No, you are quite
right to ask. My behavior must have seemed odd. It
is just that had I stayed there I think I must have tried
to thrash the blacksmith."

"Why?"

"Perhaps you did not notice, but I saw signs of
bruises on his wife's face. I can not abide bullies, and
it seems to me he must be one if he would strike a
woman so much smaller than himself. Unless, of
course, you will tell me I have mistaken the matter?"

She looked away, then back at him again. "No, you did not," she said. "I, too, have reason to believe he beats her. I can see no way to stop it, but I have often felt the same wish to thrash the fellow. Only I," Miss Barlow added with a wry smile, "should be likely to have much less success in trying to do so than you would."

For a moment he could picture her flying at the blacksmith in a rage and he worried what would happen to her. But the image also made him smile.

"You care a great deal about the tenants, don't you?" he asked.

"I have known them all my life," she said simply. "By an accident of birth my life is different from theirs, but I can imagine all too easily how I might have been born one of them."

He could not at once answer her, and she mistook his silence. Her chin came up in a gesture of defiance he was coming to recognize.

"I know you will think I should not say such things. Nor think them either. But I do. My mother taught me, before she died, to have a care for others and to picture myself in their shoes."

"How old were you when she died?" he asked.

"Twelve."

The word was almost a whisper, and for a moment her face was that of a young child, frightened, grieving, and all alone, for he could not believe her father had ever taken the time to comfort her.

"I'm sorry," he said. "I lost my parents very young as well and therefore know something of how you feel."

She did not trouble to hide her feelings then, not when she knew he must share them. "It was hard. My father never wanted girls and never ceased to curse his luck in failing to have any sons. He didn't know what to do with my sisters and me, so he took himself off to London, leaving us to the care of a governess. Then, when we were of age, he brought each of us, in turn, to London for a Season. We were to marry, you see. Advantageously, of course. All the better if it was to someone to whom he owed a great deal of money. But we could not stomach such a fate, not any of us three. And in the end we each returned to Henley Hall spinsters, for Father would not waste the funds to give any of us more than one Season. Not when we, as he put it, made such a muddle of things."

"Did you find no one to your taste?" Stamford asked, curious.

"We might have done so, had we tried," Miss Barlow acknowledged. "But it seemed to each of us that to be tied to a man, as our mother was tied to our father, would be worse than any alternative. We had no notion that he would gamble away everything, including Henley Hall, and leave us utterly penniless."

This last was said with such bitterness that Stamford flinched. And yet he could not blame her. He would have been bitter too had his alternatives been so circumscribed. He was about to say something of the sort when a shout went up in the woods ahead of them, and they both spurred their horses forward to discover what was the matter.

Chapter 6

One could not precisely race the horses through the woods, but Sir Robert and Alexandra rode as swiftly as was practical. In moments they reached the clearing from which the cry had come. There they found a child and a man, the man holding a stick and about to strike the child with it.

Before Stamford could stop her, Miss Barlow nudged her horse forward between the man and the child, and the blow that was meant for the child struck her horse instead. Instantly, the creature reared and threw his rider. Alex fell, striking her head against a tree as her horse bolted out of sight. The child rushed to her side, and the man began to bluster.

"Didn't mean to strike 'er 'orse! It were meant fer the brat, it were. T'weren't my fault, you could see it weren't, couldn't you?" he appealed to Stamford.

Robert spared no time to answer the fellow. He was too busy kneeling by Miss Barlow's side, the reins to his horse thrust into the child's willing hands.

She lay alarmingly still, and the child's words echoed his own fears. "Is she going to be all right?"

"I don't know," Stamford told the child.

"If she ain't, it's all yer fault!" the other man growled at the boy.

Now Stamford rounded on the man, worried about Miss Barlow, but needing to protect the child as well. "Shut up!" he roared. "If Miss Barlow is hurt, the blame falls directly on you! How dare you strike her horse? How dare you try to strike this child?"

" 'e's me brat," the man protested. "Ran away, 'e did. I've only now found 'im, and I mean to take 'im 'ome with me and make 'im sorry 'e ever gave me so much trouble."

Robert looked from the child's pale and frightened face to Miss Barlow, to the man, and his own expression hardened. "The child goes nowhere with you," he said. Reaching into his purse, he pulled out a coin and tossed it to the man. "I've a mind to hire him," he told the fellow. "That should compensate you for his loss."

But suddenly the child was a precious son and worth far more than one coin, and the fellow began to whine. Stamford looked at the man with narrowed eyes. He had to resolve this quickly and see to Miss Barlow's care.

"Is he? Very well, then give me back the coin and take the boy. He took my fancy, but if he means so much to you, take him home and give me back the coin."

The child flinched, and only Robert's hand on his thin shoulder kept him from running away. But Stamford had gauged his mark precisely right. The fellow stopped whining and backed away himself hastily. "No, keep the boy. Keep 'im as long as you want."

Then, before Stamford could demand the coin back again, the man fled the clearing and Robert could feel the relief in the boy's body. "You'll be safe with us," he told the child. "But you must help me now with the lady."

"Miss Barlow," the child said.

"Yes. Do you know where we can wet my handkerchief to try to bring her around?"

"There be a stream nearby," the boy offered eagerly.

"Good. Wet my handkerchief thoroughly and bring it back here as quickly as you can."

The boy took it and ran. Stamford settled himself with Miss Barlow's head in his lap. It worried him that she had not yet come around. Fortunately, the boy was back quickly and Sir Robert was able to press the cold, wet cloth against her temple where a nasty bruise was already forming. At his touch, she began to moan and thrash about.

"Hush! It's all right. You're safe. The child is safe. I am here, and I shall take care of you."

Stamford said the words in soothing tones, hoping it would calm Miss Barlow and it did. She ceased to thrash about and slowly opened her eyes. She looked up at him, her gaze unguarded for perhaps the first time since he had arrived at Henley Hall. And she smiled. It was just a smile and should have mattered not at all, but Robert found it did.

"The boy?" she asked, starting to rise and look about.

"Safe. I sent his father away. The boy will come back to Henley Hall with us."

Then she asked what seemed to Stamford to be the oddest of questions. "Why?"

"Because no child deserves to be beaten like that," he said, not even noticing how his voice had turned harsh and his expression bleak and forbidding.

But apparently she noticed and so did the child who moved a step or two away. But Miss Barlow merely smiled all the more and closed her eyes as she murmured, "Good. He will just be one more."

Robert wanted to ask what she meant by that odd remark, but he knew it was far more important to get her back to Henley Hall and send for the nearest physician. With the boy's help and her own weak attempts to cooperate, Stamford managed to seat Miss Barlow on his horse and swing himself up behind her. He gave the boy directions to follow and somehow trusted the lad would come.

Just as he was about to ride on ahead, Stamford paused to ask the boy, "What is your name? I shall need to tell the head groom whom to expect."

"John, me lord."

"Well, John, go to the stables when you reach the estate. The head groom will be expecting you."

It was an awed but soft "Thank you" that sped Stamford and his burden on their way. And oddly enough it touched him in a way that the ceremony that had raised him to baronet had not.

But he had no time to dwell on such an absurd thought. It took all his concentration to guide the horse down a path he scarcely knew and keep Miss Barlow from sliding off. He was all too conscious of how tightly his arm held her, and the soft curves that pressed against him as he did.

The moment he reached the stable yard, the head groom rushed forward to help. He reached up to take Miss Barlow from Stamford. "We've been watching for you, sir. Ever since the horse come back without her rider. Thrown, were she?"

Robert nodded. "Yes, but it wasn't her fault. She was trying to protect a child."

"That be Miss Barlow, all right," the head groom confirmed as he set her on her feet. "Never a thought to her ownself, only for them."

"Hush!" Miss Barlow said, reaching out to steady herself. "Not another word! How is the mare?"

"Well enough," the groom grumbled. "But I misliked seeing her come back without you."

"I misliked it myself," Miss Barlow retorted, managing a smile. She turned to look at Robert. "The child? Where is he? You did not let him stay unprotected with that man, did you?"

Stamford smiled reassuringly. He could not help himself. Nor stop himself from taking her hand as well. "No, I did not. Do you not remember? I told him to come here, to present himself to the head groom for work. His name, by the way," he turned to tell the man, "is John."

"Very good, sir. What do you be wishful I should do with him when he comes? Put him to work in the stables?"

Stamford frowned. "Perhaps. But not just yet. Give him a day or two to recover from his bruises. Then I shall speak to him and see where he best might suit."

"Very good, sir," the head groom told Stamford, exchanging a very odd look with Miss Barlow.

So they thought him daft, did they? Too bad! It was his estate now, and he would do as he chose. And if he chose to put up a child for a bit without putting the lad to work, well, that was just what he would do.

Miss Barlow swayed then, and he realized she looked very pale—too pale for his comfort. "Come, Miss Barlow," he said aloud. "We must go up to the house, and I shall send for a surgeon to see to your head."

"No!"

He stopped, startled at her protest. She hesitated, then said firmly, "There is a woman, a healer—she is the one we send for when anyone is hurt. The nearest surgeon is a good distance away and like as not you'd find him drunk. He generally is by ten in the morning. I should rather trust myself to Margaret in the woods."

"I see. And how do I find this, er, Margaret in the woods?"

"You don't," she told him bluntly. Then, as he drew his brows together in a frown, ready to give her a setdown, she disarmed him by saying, "Margaret doesn't like men, you see. At least we think she doesn't," Miss Barlow amended. "But she will come if Tessa goes and fetches her. In any event, my sister knows the way, and it will be faster to send her than to try to explain how to find her."

Robert wanted to shake her, but she was patently too weak for that. And what did it matter anyway if he went for the woman or if her sister did? This Margaret in the woods would have to deal with him when she came to the house to see to Miss Barlow. He could confront her prejudices then. For now his chief concern must be Miss Barlow's welfare, and anything that caused her to become this agitated must be accounted unacceptable.

"Very well, I shall send your sister for this woman. But I cannot do so until I get you up to the house."

She ceased to argue then and even allowed herself to lean on him as they went. He would have carried her, but he did not think she would let him. Still, he found he liked having her lean against him. It felt right in a way he could not explain and did not mean to even try. For one thing, it made him distinctly uncomfortable to realize the direction his thoughts were taking.

But his resolution lasted only as far as the upper lawn. There her knees began to buckle, and he caught her just in time. Over her protests he swung Miss Barlow up into his arms and carried her with swift strides toward the house.

"Hush!" he commanded. "I do not wish to drop you. No, nor have to explain to your sisters how I allowed you to collapse all but in sight of the door. I should have carried you the entire distance from the stables, but since I did not, I shall have my way now."

With his foot he pushed open the door to the kitchens and, ignoring the alarmed cries of the staff, strode through the passageway toward the main part of the house. Over his shoulder he told an astonished Potter, "Fetch Miss Barlow's sisters! At once! And some tea."

Potter hastened to do as he was bid, and within minutes both younger sisters were crowded around Miss Barlow, who was disposed on a sofa in the front parlor. Despite her pallor her voice was firm as she gave her own instructions.

"Tessa, you must go to Margaret. Ask her if she will come and see me. Tell her I was thrown from my horse and struck my head a sufficient blow to daze me for some time. Lisbeth, you must go up to my room and find the jar of willow bark that Margaret gave me. Take a small portion and ask Cook to brew some tea with it. It will help until Margaret can come and see to me herself."

They did as they were bid—no protests, no questions—as if this sort of thing happened all the time. When he was once again alone with her, Robert could not entirely keep the amusement out of his voice as he said, "Do you often doctor yourself? Or others in this household?"

She looked at him as though he were wanting in wits. "Well, of course I do!" she said. "Who else is there to see to the welfare of the family or servants or tenants except Margaret and, when she cannot come, myself? Did your mother never nurse you when you were ill?"

He turned away abruptly, unable to face or answer her. Over his shoulder he said, "I will not speak about my family, and I should be grateful if you ceased to ask such things of me. Is that understood?"

"Perfectly." It was her voice that held amusement now, but also sympathy. "I must guess that your fortune was no better than mine in how you found yourself as a child."

"Worse."

Had he spoken aloud? Robert mused. Was that his own voice so sharp with anger and hurt? He found it unthinkable, and so drew in a deep breath and waited for her to press him. But she did not. And in the end he could not help but turn to look at her, to see her expression. It was as thoughtful as he had ever seen it, but carefully schooled to reveal nothing of her thoughts, a circumstance for which he was grateful.

He didn't know how long he stared at her, the bleakest of looks in his eyes as he compared the childhood she must have had to his own, as he envied all the things he had never known and which must have seemed so natural to her.

Apparently, his expression revealed more than he wished, for she said, "I am sorry."

And because Stamford did not dare ask her what

she saw or was sorry for, he abruptly turned and
strode from the room without answering her. Instead,
he almost collided with Miss Elizabeth Barlow in the
narrow doorway. She carried a pot of tea and a cup
on a tray. How the devil had she managed that so
swiftly? Or had he been alone with Miss Barlow
longer than he realized?

In any event he ought to be grateful she was here,
he thought savagely. Miss Barlow would have no need
of him if her sister was there to attend her. He, meanwhile, would try to forget the emotions her words had
roused in him by going to the library and pondering
what he had seen.

Perhaps he ought to go through the books the late
Lord Henley had left behind as well. Surely there was
something he could salvage about this estate that he
could, in the end, give to Miss Barlow and her sisters.
It was certain he was not going to wish to return once
he was able to leave, and they could use whatever
help he could give them. After all, it had never been
his plan to win the estate from Henley in the first
place!

Chapter 7

Tessa glanced from time to time at the older woman walking by her side. They said in the village that Margaret was a witch. Tessa didn't believe in witches, not really. And Alex swore she was only a woman skilled in the ways of healing. She also said Margaret had been a friend to their mother. That certainly ought to count for something; Tessa just wasn't sure how much.

In any event, Margaret was the only healer Tessa had ever known. She'd nursed the three Barlow sisters through more than one bout of inflammation of the lungs over the years. So Tessa ought to have been comfortable with her. And perhaps she would have been if the old woman hadn't insisted on asking her when she meant to leave for London. London! As if there were any chance she would ever go to that city again. Granted, she had copied out one of her stories in her clearest hand and sent it off to a publisher in London, but who knew what would come of that? And even if it was published, that didn't mean she would go to the city.

Still, she oughtn't to worry about that now. She ought to be thinking about poor Alex—and wondering how she came to be hurt. A child, of course. It had to be a child. Well, she supposed she would find out when Alex explained to Margaret as Margaret was bound to insist she do.

Fortunately, Henley Hall came into sight a few moments later. Margaret paused to look at the edifice, an odd look upon her face. "So much unhappiness those walls have seen," she said. "But not for much longer. Oh, there'll be tragedy, there always is, but laughter too, I'll be bound. And it's about time."

The older woman looked at Tessa and grinned. "You think I'm mad, I suppose. Or a witch, like some in the village. I'm neither, of course." She paused and looked at Tessa. "Most people go through life scarcely noticing anything around them. I notice, or try to notice, everything. And so it seems to some as if I have uncanny powers. But the truth is, I put my faith in knowledge. I am not even certain I believe in magic. I just know to keep my wits about me, and that's not a fault many will forgive. Particularly not in a woman. Remember that when you go to London."

"I am not—" Tessa broke off in exasperation. What was the point of arguing? "Please, let's just go in and see my sister," she said instead.

The older woman nodded. "Yes, her head will be hurting terribly by now. Unless, of course, she still had some of the willow bark by her."

"She did. She asked for Lisbeth to brew her some tea with it," Tessa confirmed.

"Good. She'll make a good healer herself one of these days. Not like me, of course. She's not likely to ever live in the woods as I have. Or want to spend her life alone. But she'll know how to tend to her children when they're ill and the servants and tenants as well."

Tessa didn't bother to argue. Instead, she led the way inside and to the parlor, where Alex still lay on the sofa. Her coloring was better, and Tessa felt a little of the fear leaving her.

Margaret moved forward. She greeted Lisbeth with a nod, but took hold of Alex's wrist. She did several other things, none of which Tessa understood but which Alex bore quite patiently—as she did the questions. She told her story calmly and, as Tessa had guessed, there was indeed a child involved. The surprise was that Sir Robert had rescued the child and told him to come to Henley Hall. Tessa found herself warming to the thought of his kindness.

In the end the older woman nodded and said, "You'll do. Take some of the tea of the willow bark every few hours, but no more often than that. You were dazed longer than I like, but seem well enough now. I'll stay the night though, just to be sure."

The three sisters looked at one another, hesitated, and it was Alex who said, "If you stay, Margaret, you are likely to encounter Sir Robert Stamford. He is the new master here and has been in residence since yesterday."

"I know that well enough," Margaret answered in a dry voice. "The villagers are eager to pass along such news to me. It does not matter. I'll dine in the kitchen with your cook. There's a salve I promised her for her hands that I must deliver to her anyway. And then I'll spend the night in your room. I doubt I'll even see the fellow."

"On the contrary, I consider it absolutely necessary that I meet the person in whose hands Miss Barlow's health resides," a voice said from the doorway.

The three sisters glanced up in alarm at Stamford and then swiftly at Margaret. The older woman took her time, however, in turning to see who had spoken. Nor did she seem in the least dismayed to see him standing there. She lifted an eyebrow and regarded him in a manner calculated to reduce him to the state of a nervous schoolboy. He did not even flinch.

No one expected what came next. Margaret marched up to him and gently touched one side of his face, then the other. She frowned. She regarded the smile that tugged unwillingly at the corners of his mouth. She smiled herself.

"Not a regular one, are you?" she asked. And then, without waiting for an answer, she added, "You won't find what you came here looking for, but what you'll find will be something far better. I only hope you have the wits to value what you find."

And then, without waiting for a reply, she pushed past him and headed down the hallway in the direction of the kitchens. No one thought or wished to try to stop her.

Sir Robert stood frozen, unable to move. Who the devil was this woman, and what had she meant by those strange words? he wondered. Could she possibly, could anyone possibly, have guessed why he was here? But even if she had, what could she have meant by such a cryptic statement? Not find what he was seeking? That would mean their informant was wrong about where the children were being sent. But if that were so, how would this old woman have even known what he was looking for?

No, it made no sense, none of it. The woman was clearly touched in the head or, more likely, wishing to sound important, that was all. Easy to guess he would have hoped to find something here, even if it was only money from Henley's estate. Easy to guess there was none. No, the old woman was only spouting nonsense. Stamford only hoped, for Miss Barlow's sake, that Margaret's healing skills were better than her fortune-telling ones.

Dinner was, as might be expected, a somewhat strained affair. Margaret stared at him throughout the meal in the most unnerving way. He wanted to ask what she was doing there, instead of eating in the kitchen with the servants, as she had said she would do, but he didn't quite dare. In any event, he was too worried about Miss Barlow's health to cavil over such an unimportant matter.

Miss Barlow still looked pale. And she seemed to lack the quickness of tongue he had come to expect from her. As for her sisters, it was obvious that they shared his concern. They cast any number of worried looks her way, and the middle sister went so far as to suggest that Miss Barlow retire to bed directly after she ate. That she agreed without the slightest protest was enough to alarm all of them. Indeed, it was a measure of that alarm that all of them were greatly relieved the woman from the woods meant to stay the night in her room with Miss Barlow.

Perhaps it was not surprising that the other Barlow sisters also declined his company and sought their beds early. Still sleep, for Stamford, was not going to come easily that night and he knew it.

In the end, he took his candle and went down to the library in search of a book that might help put him to sleep. He found one readily enough, for Lord Henley had not wasted his blunt on novels or other entertaining literature. His taste ran to the classics a gentleman was expected to possess and every book published on horses, or so it seemed.

With one of these hopefully sleep-inducing tomes in hand, Robert went back to his room. That was what he intended, at any rate. He never could explain, not then and certainly not later, the impulse that caused him to pause outside Miss Barlow's bedroom door.

He didn't mean to knock, for that would have been foolish. But he found himself listening, anyway, wondering if she was all right. Wanting to know. And yet, he was entirely unprepared when the door suddenly opened and he found himself confronted by the woman from the woods.

"Well, come in!" she said, holding the door wide open for him.

The gasp of protest from Miss Barlow mirrored his own. Margaret would have none of it. "What are you afraid of?" she demanded. "Propriety? I am here to see that everything stays nice and proper."

"But she is in bed," he finally managed to say.

"So she is," the older woman agreed. "And needing to apologize for causing you trouble today. Come, sir, you will set her mind at ease enough for her to rest if you will only let her do so."

Fascinated, Robert found himself entering the

room. It wasn't proper, no matter what the woman said, and well he knew it. And yet somehow he could not seem to stop himself. Not even when he saw Miss Barlow propped against the pillows, lit by the candles on either side of her bed.

He had never seen her hair down before, he realized. No, nor seen her blush in just such a way. She was stammering something about not wanting to apologize after all, but he couldn't pay attention to the words. Instead, he smiled, feeling a trifle bewitched, and came to sit in the chair so conveniently placed beside her bed.

"You needn't distress yourself, you know," he said in soothing tones, taking the hand she reached out in an attempt to ward him off. "I don't mean to tease you or ask for an apology. I know what you did was right, but I do wish you had not managed to get yourself injured doing so."

Miss Barlow blushed again. Was this the woman who thought she would forever be an old maid? Utter nonsense! he thought. Impossible! Not with those deep green eyes and that halo of blond hair about her head.

Robert must have spoken aloud, for now she was blushing more than ever and looking utterly, beautifully confused. He lifted her hand to his lips and kissed it. He could not recall ever doing such a thing before, but it seemed right, somehow, here and now.

"You are foolish beyond permission," she said crossly. "Bewitched, no doubt, by some spell Margaret has cast. You cannot think me beautiful."

He tilted his head to one side. "Oh, but I do," he said. "And if I am bewitched, may it last forever."

Miss Barlow snatched her hand away, and he only chuckled. He wanted to soothe her, to tell her it didn't matter. But she wouldn't have listened to him. Not now, not yet.

Something in her eyes warned Robert she was afraid of getting hurt. Something that warned him it would be like coaxing a wild creature to get her to trust him. And some answering spark in his own breast that told him he would, he must, find a way to do so.

"You needn't be afraid of me," he said softly. "This is madness, I know, and in the morning perhaps we both shall regret such madness. But right now, in this moment, I cannot bring myself to do so."

And then, before Miss Barlow could protest, indeed before Robert even truly knew himself what he intended, he leaned forward and kissed her on the lips. It was as sweet as anything he could have imagined. And her hand clung to his now as though she would never let go. Somewhere, at the back of his mind, he knew this was impossible, he knew he was breaking every rule ever drilled into him, but he could not stop. Not, that is, until Margaret's voice broke into both their reveries.

"Enough is enough! That will do nicely, my good sir. Now off with you to your own cold, lonely bed. My lady needs her rest."

And before he even knew what was happening, Robert found himself back out in the hall, wondering if what he remembered had really just happened or whether he was dreaming, standing here outside her door.

While he was still trying to make up his mind, the door opened once again and a book was thrust into his hands. The book he had gone downstairs to find. The book he had let drop to the floor when he kissed Miss Barlow.

Horrified to discover it was no fantasy or half-waking dream, Stamford fled to his room, praying that by morning both he and Miss Barlow might both have forgotten what had passed between them.

But his treacherous body would not forget, nor his mind either. It was some time before he slept, and even then his dreams were not in the least restful. So full of turmoil were they that when he heard the scream it took him some moments to realize it was real and not part of the fantasy in which he was trapped.

Chapter 8

The scream came again, and this time Stamford was fully awake, fully aware of what it was he was hearing. And it sounded very much like a child. He threw back the covers, lit a candle, and hastily donned some clothes. This time, he vowed, he was going to discover the source of the scream. And no one was going to persuade him it was a ghost!

The scream had come from the east wing, of that he was certain. But when he reached that wing, all was silence again. There was, to be sure, a moaning sound, but he recognized it as the wind blowing through the eaves. Of a child there was no sound or sight.

Slowly, he began to pad down the hallway in his bare feet, trying each door in turn. All were empty. It was when he reached for the handle of the fourth door that a sound came from farther down the hall. Instantly, he whirled to see who it was.

Elizabeth, the youngest Barlow sister, stood there in her night shift and a wrapper. She held no candle, and while her eyes were wide open, she seemed not to see or hear him when he demanded, "What the devil are you doing out of bed?"

She ignored his words and started to move past. He reached out a hand to touch her arm, and she screamed. It was not precisely the same as the screams he had heard before. At least he didn't think so. But she had come from deeper in the east wing. And perhaps muffled by his door, this was what he had heard.

He opened his mouth to ask, then suddenly she blinked at him, opened her eyes wider still, and pulled her arm free as she hastily backed several steps away.

"What are you doing here?" she demanded. "What am I doing here? I wasn't walking in my sleep again, was I? I didn't cry out, as I usually do, did I?"

Bewildered and wishing only to calm her, Robert spoke in soft and soothing accents. "I heard a sound and came to see what it was. I am afraid you were walking in your sleep and may have cried out. Please let me escort you back to your room. You have no candle."

He held out a hand to her, but she would not take it. Instead, she stared at him for a long moment and then slowly nodded. "Yes, perhaps it would be best if I shared the light of your candle. It is so very dark in this hallway, is it not."

He didn't try to speak, afraid of frightening or embarrassing her more than she patently was. Instead, he smiled reassuringly and started slowly back toward the west wing. She fell into step beside him.

"You won't tell my sisters, will you?" she asked. "They would only worry, you see, and I would not have that for the world."

He hesitated. "Perhaps it would help if they knew?"

She shook her head vehemently. "This has happened before, and each time they found me they were most distressed. Even Margaret, from the woods, had no answer as to what might help cure me. And since there is no answer, I must wish to spare my sisters what worry I can."

He could only applaud her wish even though he felt a strong desire to help. He didn't like to see her looking so distressed.

But they were at her doorway by now, and he waited until she slipped inside, then padded the rest of the way to his own room. His mind would not let go of what he had just seen. Was the youngest sister the source of the scream he had heard? Perhaps, perhaps not. And if she was not the source of the scream, if he had been right that it had been a child, then what should he do?

Briefly Robert considered going back and checking the rest of the east wing. But if someone was hiding a child there, they would have had ample time to move to a safer spot, and they would surely have done so by now. It was unlikely he could find the child tonight, even if there was a child, so he realized he might as well go back to bed.

At least all the other doors remained closed. He had no wish to try to speak with the middle sister at this hour, nor did he wish to risk any repetition of what had happened earlier with the eldest.

As he undressed, Robert wondered what he should say to the Barlow sisters in the morning about the youngest. Should he tell the older ones what he had seen and heard? Or should he do as Elizabeth asked and keep her secret? It was a dilemma that still occupied his mind as he slipped into sleep a short time later.

"You were supposed to lock his door!" Lisbeth hissed at her eldest sister over the breakfast table. "Now he is halfway to thinking me most eccentric. I had to pretend I was walking in my sleep!"

"Yes, well, you may recall that I was laid up in my bed and guarded by Margaret last night," Alex replied in acid tones. "I did not have the chance to go and lock his door. One of you ought to have thought to check."

"It's absurd to argue over it now," Tessa interceded. "What happened, happened. And it might have been worse if he had tried his door and found it locked. How clever of you, Lisbeth, to beg him not to speak of it to us. That ought to utterly confuse him. But what are we to do about the children?"

"I told him it was a ghost crying out," Alex offered, reaching for another cup of tea.

"And did he believe you?" Lisbeth demanded.

The eldest Barlow sister smiled wryly. "No. I think your tale of sleepwalking far superior and more plausible. As, no doubt, did he. Tessa is right. So long as the children keep crying out at night, sooner or later he is bound to discover our secret."

"Well, at least until we think of somewhere else to place them, we must make certain his door is locked at night!"

"And if he discovers that we are locking him into his room?"

Alex stared into her cup of tea. "I think," she said, her voice not entirely steady, "after Margaret's trick last night, he will not wonder that I should feel unsafe with us three and him alone on the same floor."

All three sisters smiled at one another, for she had already told them the story. It was a smile that Stamford would have found most unnerving. Indeed, he did find it so, walking into the breakfast parlor at just that moment.

Lisbeth promptly fled the room, a circumstance that did not seem to surprise the man. Tessa and Alex looked at each other, wondering just how much he had overheard. But he seemed oblivious to the undercurrents in the room. He greeted them, proceeded to fill his plate from the sideboard, and then came to sit with them as though nothing were out of the ordinary.

Alex eyed him surreptitiously as she sipped her tea. She could not help remembering how he had looked at her last night when Margaret called him into her room.

Apparently his thoughts marched in tune with hers, for abruptly he looked around and then said with a frown, "Where is Margaret? The healer?"

"She went back to the woods early this morning," Alex replied. "She does not like this house, it seems. Once she was certain I had taken no permanent harm, she left."

He nodded to himself as he speared a piece of ham

on his plate. "She is," he observed dryly, "a most
unconventional, a most unusual woman. How do you
come to know her?"

"Everyone knows her hereabouts," Tessa answered.

"But you said she held a locket of your mother's
for you?" he persisted.

Alex drew in a deep breath. "It would seem our
mother and Margaret were dear friends. I never knew
that until after Mama died. But my mother was always
curious, always wanting to learn about plants and healing, so I suppose it was a natural friendship."

"Just as yours is now," he hazarded shrewdly. "You
also are curious about plants and healing, are you
not?" She stiffened, and he added, carelessly, "Oh, I
make no protest. Indeed, I consider it both admirable
and convenient, given that you have no physician close
at hand."

She wanted to dislike the man, she truly did. But
he had a way of disarming her defenses. How dare he
understand? How dare he sound so sympathetic?

And because feeling this way distressed her so, Alex
made her voice tart as she replied, "Oh, I make no
doubt you find it convenient to have a housekeeper
able to minister to your household, should any one of
them fall ill."

He was not put out of countenance, as she had half
hoped he would be. Instead, he smiled at her and said
in a kind voice that unnerved her more than ever,
"That is not what I meant, but let it pass. Tell me
instead, how long has your sister suffered these spells
of sleepwalking?"

Her jaw fell open; she could not stop it. And she
knew her shock was mirrored on Tessa's face as well.
Indeed, her younger sister blurted out, "But she asked
you not to tell us, didn't she?"

The moment the words were out of Tessa's mouth,
she knew her mistake. She colored up fiercely and
turned her gaze to Alex, as though expecting her to
rescue the situation. Which, of course, she did.

"My sister is astonished that Lisbeth confided in you. We have each encountered Lisbeth sleepwalking, of course, and she has always begged us not to tell the other. And, like you, we have always done so anyway. I collect you encountered my sister last night, walking in her sleep?"

"In the east wing, without a candle," Stamford agreed grimly.

"Oh, we do not allow her a candle at night. Otherwise she might set something on fire when she walks in her sleep," Tessa improvised. "The maid removes it once Lisbeth is tucked up into her bed."

Sir Robert lowered his eyes to his plate, and neither sister could guess what he was thinking. When the silence stretched on, it was Alex who once more took up the tale.

"You must not be thinking my sister is a danger, for she is not. It is more worrisome than anything else. When we anticipate that she might be restless at night, we are careful to stay, one of us, with her. But we did not guess she would be last night."

"I see."

Did he? How much did he see and how clearly? Alex dearly wished she knew the answer to these two questions. But of course she could not ask.

"Will you walk with me this morning, Miss Barlow?" Stamford asked. "I should like to see the gardens. You said they needed pruning, and I should like to see them more closely to decide what I must do to bring them up to snuff."

The way he looked at her set her pulse racing. It could not mean what it felt like it meant, but still Alex found it most disconcerting. Perhaps that was why she sought refuge in what formality she could.

"Of course, Sir Robert."

"Shall I come, too?" Tessa asked brightly.

"No."

Just that one word from him, curt and uncompromising. Alex tried to soften the blow to her sister's feelings. "You were going to see to things upstairs today, weren't you?" she said with some meaning.

Tessa blinked. And then she understood. They had to find a safer place to hide the children. And while Alex had Sir Robert out looking at the gardens, that would be the perfect time to move them. So now she nodded. "Yes, of course. I had forgotten."

"What do you need to do upstairs?" Sir Robert asked politely.

Tessa stared at him, unable for a moment to answer. Alex did so for her. In a voice that was surprisingly placid, she replied, "My sister needs to inspect the linens and then see to all the hangings in the rooms we no longer use. It is always wise to know what must be replaced and what will suffice for another year or more."

He stared at her. "You are remarkably efficient."

"Isn't that what you wish? Surely you would not be pleased with a housekeeper who neglected such basic responsibilities?"

"No, of course not."

In the awkward silence that followed, Alex was able to nod at her sister to go. She must at least pretend to be inspecting the linens until after they were out of the house. Let Sir Robert see her at such a mundane pursuit and he was unlikely to suspect she was guilty of doing or plotting anything else.

When the silence continued to stretch on, Alex rose to her feet. "I know you will excuse me. I need to speak with Cook. When you are ready to inspect the garden, you may find me in the kitchens."

He nodded a curt dismissal that oddly hurt. What, after all, did she expect? He was her employer, and she was merely his housekeeper. Nor should she want any warmer feelings from Sir Robert than he had already shown her, Alex told herself firmly. It would be far too dangerous.

However much Stamford might like her, Alex found it hard to imagine that his regard would extend to the children under her care. He was far more likely, despite his rescue of the boy yesterday, to insist that she send them away.

No, she ought to be grateful, Alex told herself, that Sir Robert had retreated into himself. And she must remember from this moment forward to do the same. She did not want him, after all, to feel too comfortable here, for then he might stay and they would all be in the suds!

Chapter 9

Stamford wondered just what mischief the Barlow sisters were engaged in. He did not believe the story about linens and hangings. But neither could he quite bring himself to believe they were the persons he was looking for. These three women? Behind the kidnapping of children? For what possible purpose? A man like Henley, yes—Robert could imagine him exploiting children if it suited his plans. But not the three Barlow sisters.

Perhaps it was simply his imagination. He had, after all, not had an uninterrupted night of sleep since he arrived at Henley Hall. And that could only add to his grim mood and naturally suspicious nature.

Still, there was something that had felt not quite right about finding Miss Elizabeth Barlow apparently walking in her sleep last night in the east wing. It felt even less right in the light of morning.

Sir Robert took his time going to fetch the eldest Miss Barlow. Let her grow impatient waiting. Perhaps if her temper was roused, she might let slip something. Not that he had any great hopes for such a thing, but it was possible.

She was indeed in a temper when, an hour and a half later, he finally strolled into the kitchen and asked her if she was ready to walk in the gardens now.

"I thought," she said in acid accents, "you must have changed your mind."

"No, no," he said soothingly, "only my neck cloth.

It wasn't tied quite right, you see, and it took me a dozen efforts before I could succeed."

Since his cravat looked precisely as it had when she had seen him at breakfast, it is perhaps not surprising that she snorted in disgust and said, "Of all the ways of roasting me that you might try, telling me you are in effect a dandy is the one tale I cannot swallow whole. Recollect, sir, that you told me you do not travel with your valet. And any man who does not travel with a valet cannot persuade me he considers the tying of his cravat to be of greater importance than walking in the garden!"

He had to work hard to suppress the smile that threatened to light up his face. But he managed to keep his expression bland as he said, "My dear Miss Barlow, do you really think it wise to question your employer's veracity in such a blatant way?"

She colored up a fiery red at that, and Stamford found himself thinking that for all her talk of being his housekeeper, she really had not accustomed herself to the change in her circumstances. If she had, she would not have expected to sit down to dinner with him as if it were still her house and he the guest. Nor would she have had her sisters join them. He wondered when it would occur to her to wonder why he allowed it.

He also wondered what would become of the Barlow sisters when his work here was done—and if there was any way he could help them. Assuming, that is, that she and her sisters were not involved in the disappearance of the children. For if they were, then however much he was drawn to her, Stamford would see that she suffered the full penalty of the law. He could not abide people who exploited children. And in his experience, there were far too many who did so and far too few times he had had the chance to even the score. Suddenly, he realized she was speaking to him.

". . . all right, Sir Robert?"

"Yes, yes," he said irritably, conscious he had been

woolgathering with all the kitchen staff to see. "You promised to show me the gardens, and I cannot comprehend why we are standing here wasting our time chattering!"

Her eyes narrowed, and he could see the effort it required for her to bite back a sharp retort. But she did so, managing to master herself so completely that her voice was entirely without any inflection as she said, "Of course. Right this way, Sir Robert."

He followed, aware that half that same kitchen staff were now looking daggers at his back and would no doubt spend the next quarter hour ripping his character to shreds. Well, he did not care if they did so. He had far more important matters to think about than whether or not he was liked.

Stamford tried to remain aloof. He really did. Miss Barlow was his employee and someone to question about the children, nothing more. That was what he told himself. But he could not help noticing how her hair kept slipping free from the pins and he kept wanting to touch it. Just as he wanted to touch the bloom in her cheeks. Nor did he miss the way her eyes softened as she pointed out her favorite portions of the garden, or rather, what would be her favorite portions when they bloomed.

She loved the roses, of course. That he could have guessed. But he wondered if he would have known about the bluebells if she hadn't told him. Or the fragrant lavender, which she said they always dried to put among the sheets in the cupboard.

When she was done, she turned to him and said in a prim and proper voice, "What will you wish to have done with the garden?"

He looked about with some bewilderment. "Hire a gardener, I suppose. Someone who can do what ought to be done. Pull the weeds. Trim back some of the bushes. How the devil should I know? I've never had to deal with a garden before."

"But surely at your other estate . . . ?"

She broke off her half-spoken protest as though remembering it was not her place to argue. He shrugged.
"The gardens were in excellent shape when I pur-
chased the place, and I have never given any further
thought to them."

Hesitantly, she asked, "But what about the home
where you grew up? What sort of gardens did your
mother plant?"

He couldn't answer her. He couldn't even begin to
try. He knew that something in his face betrayed him,
for suddenly she reached out a hand to touch his arm.
But he couldn't bear the sympathy he read in her face.
He had to say something and quickly.

"My mother had no gardens. The place where I
grew up had none. No one cared about gardens, you
see."

She didn't, of course. He could read the confusion
in her face. But he could also see that he had given
her enough setdowns this morning so that she was not
anxious for more and was not likely to press him to
explain. He drew in a deep breath. Somehow he had
to give her thoughts a new direction.

"That I did not grow up with gardens does not
mean I cannot learn. Let us go through these once
again, and this time I promise I shall pay more attention as you tell me what grows where and what you
think I should do to alter their condition."

It answered. It answered very well. So well that
when they went back into the house, some time later,
they were on cordial terms once again. At least they
were until he saw the child scampering up the stairs.
The boy, perhaps six and certainly no older, was a
stranger to Robert, but one look at his companion and
it was clear to him that Miss Barlow knew precisely
who the boy might be.

He looked at her, one eyebrow raised, silently asking her to explain and fervently hoping she could. Miss
Barlow drew in a breath and then seemed to give
herself a shake. In a firm voice, one that only qua-

vered slightly, she said, "Tom! What are you doing there? You are supposed to be helping Potter polish the silver!"

It was fascinating to watch the expressions chase themselves across the lad's face: excitement, chagrin when he saw them watching him, fear, surprise and confusion, then sudden understanding.

"Oh, aye, Mr. Potter. Polish the silver."

"That way, Tom! Through the door over there, as well you ought to know."

The lad caught on quickly, Stamford had to give him that. The question was, what was he doing here in the first place? Was he one of the children Stamford was seeking? And if so, if he were being kept a prisoner here, why had he not blurted out the truth to Robert?

To cover his confusion Stamford began to ask questions. "Is it so difficult to find servants that you must hire children?" he asked in a lazy drawl.

"At t-t-times," she stammered. "Tom is very good with s-s-silver."

"I see."

"You don't approve?" she asked anxiously.

Perhaps he ought to have prevaricated. Perhaps he ought to have pretended sympathy with her to coax her into telling him what he needed to know. But Robert could not. In the end, he put his hands behind him to hide how tightly he clasped them together.

Robert's face was a mask of rigid impassivity as he replied, "No, I do not approve. I do not believe in putting children to work so young. No doubt you think their wages easier to pay than adults, but I will not, Miss Barlow, be a party to such practices. You will hire adults or no one at all."

She looked at him in confusion. For once he could not tell what she was thinking.

"You do not wish to have children working here?" she said at last. "But you brought home the other boy yesterday and said he was to work in the stables."

"I brought him here to make certain he was safe," Robert said impatiently. "He will stay until he is a little older. Then, since he seemed to like horses, he may very well work in the stables."

"And in the meantime?" she demanded.

"Miss Barlow," Stamford said, biting off each word, "I fail to see what affair it is of yours what I choose to do with my estate. And it is my estate now, however much that reality may distress you. Now go and find Tom and send him home. At once!" he added when she still did not move.

"Y-y-yes, sir." She turned and fled, leaving Robert to seek refuge in the library.

Alex's head was in a whirl. What was she to do now? No matter what the risk, she could not send Tom away. Nor any of the other children either. For a moment, she was tempted to go to Sir Robert and tell him the truth. After all, if he had rescued one child yesterday, he might be willing to rescue the others as well.

But she could not take the chance. Not yet. Not until she saw what purpose Stamford had for the boy he'd taken under his wing. Appalling as the thought might be, more than one child brought to Alex by Margaret had been fleeing a man who liked children better than he should.

She found Tom with Potter, who was looking utterly bewildered that the boy expected to help him polish silver. The older man looked at Alex with relief.

"I'm trying to tell the boy, Miss Barlow, that we polished the silver just yesterday."

"I know," she replied soothingly. "But I had to tell Sir Robert something. Tom, what were you doing on the stairs? Didn't Miss Tessa explain how dangerous it was for the gentleman, Sir Robert, to see you here?"

"We were bored upstairs. There's nothing to do. And Miss Tessa and Miss Lisbeth were busy moving our things to different rooms," the boy protested. "And you hadn't come to see us at all."

Alex sighed. "I know. It is just until Sir Robert leaves."

"When?"

"I don't know."

"Might be he means to stay awhile," Potter said, pitching his voice low so that they could not be overheard. "His coachman told Cook that Sir Robert had to leave London, whether he wanted or no, and that he can't return until some sort of trouble blows over."

Alex closed her eyes. It only wanted that. To learn their guest, that is to say their new master, meant to stay for some time. She could hope to hide the children for a few days, perhaps even a week. But she could not see how such a deception could succeed for much longer than that.

She sank into the nearest chair, trying to think. Margaret could not and, indeed, would not take the children in for more than a day or two. There were far too many by now for her to handle by herself, even if she were willing. And there was no hope of finding homes for them any time soon or Alex would already have done so.

She let out a breath. No, she could see no way out of this coil. Not yet, at any rate. She would not, could not with the welfare of the children at stake, give up until she did see her way clear on how to protect them.

"Go upstairs," Alex told Tom. "And use the back stairs. Tell the others again how important it is to be quiet and to stay out of sight. Do you understand me?"

He nodded vigorously. She gave him a quick hug and sent him on his way. Potter eyed her and sighed lugubriously. "I see trouble ahead, Miss Barlow. Sir Robert Stamford ain't the man to forgive being deceived like this. No, nor taken advantage of, neither."

"More information from the coachman?" Alex said teasingly.

"Aye, it is," Potter agreed. "And you may pretend all you want he's wrong, but the fellow knows his master. Stands to reason he would. And he said Sir Robert has crushed men who tried to take advantage of him."

Alex rose to her feet and shook out her slightly rumpled skirt where Tom had pressed against her. "Ah, but I am not a man," she told Potter.

He eyed her gloomily. "All the more reason to worry what he might do if he discovers what you and your sisters are up to upstairs."

"Well, he shan't," Alex said firmly. "One way or another, we shall manage to keep the children safe and their existence a secret from him."

And with that she headed back to the main part of the house, but her resolution lasted only as far as the foyer. There she saw yet another child on the stairs—a little girl, Sara. She was perhaps three. She looked at Alex, and her teary face brightened with a great big smile. And before Alex could hush her, she spread her arms wide and cried out with delight, "Mama!"

And out of the corner of her eye, Alex saw Sir Robert's startled expression watching her.

Chapter 10

Miss Barlow stood frozen to the spot. "Mama!" the child called out again, more insistently this time.

Sir Robert Stamford ran possibilities in his head. Had Miss Barlow been married and widowed? But if so, why had she not told him? Or was disgrace the true reason she had retired from London unwed? That was far more likely an explanation, he decided. One did not, after all, have to hide children who were born in lawful wedlock.

He looked at the girl again. Was this child the reason Miss Barlow lived so retired in the countryside with her sisters? Was this what she was trying to hide from him? The child he had heard crying in the night? It would explain a great deal.

And why the devil didn't she go to her daughter?

"She is calling for you. Hadn't you better answer her?" he found himself asking curtly.

As though dazed, she moved toward the child, slowly at first and then much faster. She picked up the child and hushed her, stroking the child's hair with great tenderness. Robert felt a tension ease from his body as he realized he had half expected her to reject the child, to push her away, as he had been pushed away when he was little.

But no, she was as gentle, as soothing, as anyone could have wished in a mother. Her face was pale with fear, and she tried to shield the child as much as possible from his sight. Robert found he did not like her fear.

"Take the child upstairs and when she is settled pray come back down and see me in the library," he said curtly. Then, turning on his heel, he retreated to that room, shutting the door behind him.

Alex all but ran up the steps, cradling Sara against her breast. She met Lisbeth on the stairs. "Oh! There she is. I was coming to look for Sara. Tom told us that Sir Robert had seen him. What about Sara?"

Alex drew in a breath and realized that Tessa was there as well. Good. This way she would only have to tell the tale once.

"He saw Sara—and heard her call me Mama. He drew the natural conclusion, and I did not correct him."

Their eyes were wide with worried astonishment. "Is he going to throw us out?"

"Does he know about the others?"

"He will ruin you when he goes back to London and tells how Miss Barlow is a mother."

"Should we pack our bags?"

Alex answered the last question first. "No. Let us wait and see what he says. He told me to bring Sara upstairs and settle her, then to go back down and speak with him in the library."

"What are you going to tell him?" Tessa asked.

"I don't know," was Alex's honest answer.

"Shall we go with you?" Lisbeth asked bravely.

Alex smiled at her youngest sister, but shook her head. "No. I shall face him alone. Come, I refuse to panic until I must. Perhaps he will be kind and let us stay at least a little longer."

Her sisters snorted their disbelief, but they did not try to stop her. For more than ten years she had acted as a mother to both of them, and they were accustomed to doing as she said. So now they did not protest as Alex handed Sara over to Lisbeth and then turned to go back downstairs.

Alex drew in a deep breath and squared her shoulders without even knowing she did so. When she came to the library door, she paused to take another very deep breath. Then and only then did she knock, and when Sir Robert called out to her to come in, she did.

His expression was cold and drawn, implacable it seemed to Alex. He indicated she should sit on the other side of the desk from him and she did. Then she waited. She would not begin, she would not say a word until he told her what he was thinking.

"Is she settled?" he asked at last.

"Yes."

"So quickly?"

"My sisters are looking after her."

"Ah, I see." A pause, a very long one, and then he said softly, almost gently, "Why didn't you tell me?"

Alex looked down at her hands. How to answer? "Can you blame me?" she said. "How could I know whether, once you knew of her existence, you would throw me, throw all of us out of the house?"

He nodded as though it was a reasonable thing to fear. And so it was. Many men would have done so. He still might. "The father would not marry you?"

She smiled a wry smile. If he wondered at it, he did not say so. "I would not have married him in any case," she replied.

"I see. How do you intend to provide for your child?"

"So long as you let me stay here as your house-keeper, there is no difficulty," Alex said, choosing her words with great care. She did not want to have to lie to him, but she would do anything she could to protect the children. "If, or rather when, you say I must leave, then I shall have to find a way to support myself and, I hope, all my children."

"All your children?" He blinked at her. "You mean you have another?"

She looked at him, her eyes wide. Perhaps it was a mistake. Her sisters would surely say that it was. But she decided to trust Stamford.

Alex tilted up her chin. "I have roughly a dozen children, sir. They have been staying here, on your charity, though you did not know it. I could not think what else to do with them, you see, and did not think you would notice the small cost of their care. My sisters help me with them. Tessa tells them stories, and Lisbeth is their teacher. We never meant to cheat you, but their welfare seemed a matter of greater importance than your possible disapproval. Particularly as Mr. James assured us you were wealthy. Wealthy enough not to notice, we thought, the cost."

He drew in a deep breath and fought for control of his temper. Alex could see the struggle by the expressions that chased across his face. She held her own breath while she waited.

"I think," he said at last, "you had best begin at the beginning."

Her sisters would call her mad, and perhaps they would be right. But she told him. All about Margaret and the children who came to her. About the homes where she had been able to place some of them. About how the first child she could not place came to stay with her and then the others. About the blacksmith and his wife. She explained that some of the children had been rescued from abusive masters and some from abusive parents. She told him how Sara and her brother and sister had been orphaned in a fire. She explained how she could turn none of the children away.

Sir Robert kept his face impassive. She had not a clue to what he was thinking. He listened intently to what she said and asked a good many questions, most of which she could not answer. When she was done, he sat silently, staring at her face as though he could see into her very soul.

When the silence stretched on too long, she looked him in the eyes and said, "What will you do now, Sir Robert? Make us all leave, I presume."

"No!"

"No?"

She did not try to hide her relief. How could she? It was far too great. She did not understand Stamford's response. It had been instinct that led her to confide the truth in him, and she had thought herself mad to do so. But apparently that instinct had been correct.

Sir Robert rose to his feet and paced the room. A number of expressions crossed his face and Alex began to wonder if perhaps she had made a mistake. If he did not intend to make them leave, what did he have in store for them? And because she was not a woman to hide from unpalatable truths, she found herself asking aloud, "Why aren't you angry? Why don't you mean to make us leave?"

He turned and stared at her, clearly startled by her words. "You would do anything to protect those children, wouldn't you?" he said.

Alex nodded. "But you have no reason to do so."

"Don't I?" he retorted. "Tell me, what do you know of who I am?"

"I know that you are very wealthy," Alex said slowly. "And you have the reputation of being a very successful gambler, something I cannot doubt since my father lost Henley Hall to you."

"That took very little skill," Stamford replied with some bitterness. "Not when he was so far into his cups. Had he come to me the next morning, we might have reached some sort of understanding, but he did not. He shot himself instead. What else do you know about me? Come, you may be honest. Tell me the worst gossip you have heard."

"That you are a rake—someone who cares for naught but himself."

"That is all?" he demanded.

She looked at him, confused, and spread her hands wide. "What else should I have heard, sir?"

"Nothing of my origins?"

She shook her head. He seemed to debate with himself then as to whether to tell her or not. In the end he did. He came around and sat behind the desk again, his fingers steepled under his chin.

"I was born the wrong side of the blanket. Son, I am told, to some great man. I never knew who he was. No, nor my mother either. My earliest memories are of an orphanage where my parents placed me. No one could or would tell me anything of who I was or where my parents came from. Apparently, however, someone was watching. And when I reached my ninth year, I was taken out of the orphanage and sent to Harrow. You may imagine or, perhaps mercifully you cannot, what my existence was like there. Unknown son to an unknown father, the only advantage I had was having learnt to fight in my cradle and against boys who did not allow of any rules. Somehow I made friends with a fellow who is now Lord Ransley. He introduced me to the Prince of Wales when we came of age. I did the prince a single service. Just what it was I am not at liberty to say. Perhaps it was that combined with my natural father's standing, but I was made Sir Robert Stamford—and given sufficient funds to establish myself in the manner to which others thought I should. Given that good fortune combined with a knack with cards, I soon trebled that initial stake and became a fellow accepted almost everywhere in London. At least everywhere that men may gather. I have yet to be invited to any event sponsored by a lady."

He spoke carelessly, as though it mattered not a whit to him what he had had to endure. But there were moments when the corners of his mouth tightened as he strove to guard his emotions. And his eyes, if nothing else, would have given him away.

Alex doubted that he meant for anyone to know how deep the scars ran, how fresh the humiliations still were in his heart. But he could not hide any of it from her. Not when she knew only too well what it was like to be unwanted by one's own father.

It was not wise, it was not prudent, but even before

he was done with the telling she reached out and took his hand in hers. And when he was done and looked her straight in the eye, daring her to condemn or spurn him, she lifted that hand to her lips and gently kissed it with both her lips and her tears.

"You have come so far," she said in a voice choked with emotion, "and still have the capacity to feel and to care. That is a rare and wonderful thing. Anyone who cannot see your value must, I think, be accounted a fool."

He snatched his hand away then and stared as though looking for proof she was mocking him. She did not try to hide the way his words had touched her heart. She met his gaze with her own, steady and open, hiding nothing, though her hand stole up to clutch the locket at her throat.

His eyes fixed on that locket, and nervously she dropped her hand to her lap. In the end he slowly reached out, took her hand, and lifted it to his lips in a gesture that mirrored her own earlier. Then, with a voice that was husky with unspoken emotion, he looked at her and said, "Marry me, Miss Barlow. Please?"

Chapter 11

Miss Barlow knocked over her chair in her haste to back away. She looked as though she thought him mad, and if the truth be told, Robert felt a little mad himself. Thornsby would have his head for this!

What had he been thinking? What the devil had made him propose to Alexandra? And even if he did wish to marry her, what the devil made him think she might accept? Upon only two days' acquaintance? And yet how else was he to protect her? How else was he to make certain she did not suffer for trying to help these children?

He had a great many questions about the children that she still had not answered. But he had no doubt he had found what Thornsby had sent him here to discover. Only the matter was not quite what they had envisioned. The children had not been kidnapped in order to be sold or exploited elsewhere he realized, but rather to be protected. And that altered everything.

Later those questions would have to be answered, and he would have to figure out with Thornsby just what they were going to do. But that could wait. For now there was the matter of the marriage proposal he had just made. And Miss Barlow's response to it.

It was not as though it was a repugnant notion to him. But apparently it was to her. Slowly, he sat down. He understood. He really did. It was not, after all, as if this had never happened to him before.

"I see," he said, careful to keep his voice calm.

"You cannot stomach the thought, when all is said and done, of allying yourself to a bastard, no matter how well he has done for himself."

She had reached the library door by the time he was finished saying these words. She halted and turned to face him, disbelief evident upon her face.

"Is that what you believe?" Miss Barlow demanded, advancing as quickly as, moments before, she had tried to make her retreat.

Robert frowned and spread his hands. "What else could it be?" he asked in confusion.

She planted her hands on the desk, bending toward him. "I thought, sir, you were mocking me. I still believe you must have been. I am a confirmed spinster. I have traded upon your kindness by filling this house not only with my sisters without telling you, but with the children of strangers as well. I have not a penny to my name. No dowry and a reputation ruined by both eccentricity and the imprudence of my father. How am I to possibly believe you could be serious about an offer of marriage?"

Robert gave a wry and painful smile. "Because I am."

Miss Barlow sat back down in her chair, after righting it of course. She was, it seemed, disarmed by his candor. "I don't understand," she said.

Nor do I, Robert thought. Thornsby would positively have his head for this! But of course he could not say such a thing aloud. Instead, he tried to put his feelings into words, but it proved a surprisingly difficult task. He kept his eyes fixed on the locket at her throat because he could not bring himself to meet her clear, intelligent, questioning gaze. Not when he was about to lie to her.

"I am here, at this estate, because the Prince of Wales wishes me to marry," he said, repeating the story the *ton* believed to be true. "I had thought to stay until his fury waned, but there is an alternative. Marry me and I am free of his anger. Marry me and you shall have a place to stay for the rest of your life. And so will your sisters." He paused, then added the most important thing he needed to say, "The only thing I ask is that you allow me to arrange a suitable placement for the children."

"Placement for the children?" Miss Barlow echoed, bewildered. "But I have become attached to them."

Robert rose to his feet. He clasped his hands behind him and steeled himself to the task of making her agree. The children could not, must not stay here. But how could he make her understand why without telling her the truth? And he could not tell her that. Instead, he drew on part of the truth, the things he knew his friends would say.

"That is as may be," Robert said, his words clipped and his voice brisk. "But surely you see that if my purpose in marrying you is to establish myself in society, Miss Barlow, then any reminders of my background, such as the presence of these children in my household, simply will not do. You needn't worry—I shall make certain they are taken care of properly."

She tilted up her chin. "I will not abandon them."

"I am not asking you to do so," he said mildly. "I am only asking you to allow me to arrange a more suitable placement for them."

"I will not do it!"

She would not let him place the children elsewhere, or she would not marry him? Robert wasn't certain which she meant. Either way, he didn't like her answer. Ought he to press her? He knew from what he had seen of Miss Barlow that would only cause her to become more obstinate still. Better to pretend to give way and try again later. So now he shrugged.

"As you will," he said as though it were no great matter to him. He paused, then added, "I can understand that this is a notion you may need some time to consider. To accustom yourself to the idea, perhaps. Therefore I will not consider your refusal as final. At least not for the moment. But I will ask you again tomorrow. Because I should very much like to return to London and soon."

She did not at once answer him, and the silence stretched on until Robert felt he must force her to speak. When she did, her voice was so low, at first, that he had to strain to hear. But then it grew stronger as she went on.

"How flattering, sir. I should have known, indeed I did know, it could not be my person that attracted you. How convenient you make it all sound. I am to be the solution to your troubles with the Prince of Wales, and you are to be the solution to mine. Provided, of course, that I am willing to give up my children."

He slammed his hand on the desk between them. "They are not your children!" he all but shouted.

She went on as if he had not spoken. "I suppose that if I refuse, then my sisters and I must leave at once. Your future bride, whomever she may be, would not want three other women here—particularly three women who obviously do not know their place. My apologies, sir, but I cannot marry you and forgive me if I led you to believe I was desperate enough to do so. Had a convenient future been my only concern, I could have accepted any number of proposals the Season my father brought me out. But I will not, cannot do so. Not when I saw what my mother's life was like. Penury is preferable to being hostage to a man who neither respects nor likes me. Nor will I send away these children! They need more than just a place to live and food to eat. They need someone to truly care about their future. I am sorry to inconvenience you, Sir Robert, but I cannot believe you will really have such a great trouble finding a bride."

Stamford felt himself go cold, very cold. He had bungled matters very badly. He tried again, his voice almost coaxing as he said, "Must you think the worst of me? I had thought that we were in a way to becoming friends."

Perhaps if she had not spoken, he could have kept his distance. But instead she whispered, "We were."

Without thinking, he took a step toward her, reaching out a hand in her direction. But she stepped backward.

"No. Please. I cannot listen to anymore today. Tomorrow you will be grateful I did not. We can speak more later about what we are all to do and how soon my sisters and I must leave."

And then she fled the room. Robert sighed. He could not remember the last time he had been so clumsy! What was he to do now? Miss Barlow did not trust him. She had not believed him when he offered her his heart—and risked his career in doing so. Nor could he blame her. But somehow he had to retrieve matters.

And he had to figure out what he was going to tell Thornsby. This wasn't at all what they had expected. And in his heart, Robert could not help but side with the rescuers. The only trouble was, what would Thornsby say? And what about all those men who had filed reports and complaints and were demanding their property be returned?

Alex stood in the upper hallway, shaking. She must collect herself, her thoughts before she saw her sisters or the children. She must not let them see how distressed she was. And she must decide what she would tell them.

Sir Robert had said they must leave. Or, rather, he had said the children must leave, and that came to the same thing. And he had said so even before she had spurned his offer of marriage. Surely now he would mean it more than ever! They must make plans, she and her sisters. They must decide how they would look after the children.

She ought to have known her sisters would come looking for her, but she had not. She had thought they would wait until she came to them. So they found her before she was ready, and in spite of her resolution not to burden them, Alex found herself explaining everything.

"We shall have to leave here. Perhaps I could support us," Tessa said quietly.

"You?" Both Alex and Lisbeth stared at her in astonishment.

"Perhaps I could find a publisher in London for my stories," she said defensively. "I sent off a manuscript and I am waiting to hear."

"And I could become a governess," Lisbeth offered. "My needs would be met, and I could send you whatever I was paid. That would surely help."

Alex hugged both her sisters. "I am very grateful that you both wish to help. But I cannot let you, either of you, try to support all of us. I doubt it would be enough, anyway. I promise I shall think of some means to do so."

"How?" Tessa asked bluntly.

"You do not mean to accept Stamford's offer after all, do you?" Lisbeth asked suspiciously.

Alex hesitated, then gave herself a mental shake and forced herself to smile. "Of course not! The notion is patently absurd! He does not care a jot about me, and how can I marry a man who does not?"

Her sisters peered closer, too close for Alex's comfort. Her wariness was proved all too valid when Tessa said softly, "But you care for him, do you not?"

"She does!" Lisbeth crowed softly.

Alex shook her head, panic flaring through her. "No! I, that is, it does not signify, even if I did! It is absurd. He does not care for me at all. Not once did he mention such a thing. He only talked of convenience and solving both our problems."

"But he is a kind man," Tessa said thoughtfully.

"And shrewd," Lisbeth added.

"And he looks at you as if he does not entirely dislike you," Tessa chimed in again.

"Stop!" Alex held up a hand to ward off anymore

of their observations. "I have told Sir Robert that I cannot marry him and that is that. We must make other plans."

"What plans?" Tessa asked bluntly.

Alex clutched at the locket around her neck. "I wished for children and I have them," she said with a wry smile, not wanting them to know how worried she felt. "Perhaps I ought to wish for a solution to this as well."

"Why not wish for Sir Robert to love you?" Lisbeth asked earnestly. "He is right, after all, that it would solve so many problems if he did."

Still holding the locket, Alex shook her head and said, a hint of sadness in her voice, "I might as well wish for the moon as wish that Sir Robert could love me as I think I am beginning to love him."

It must have been her imagination that the locket seemed to warm beneath her touch. And it was most certainly foolish imagination that for a moment an image of herself, standing side-by-side with Stamford as they exchanged vows, flashed through her mind. It would never, surely could never, happen. After what had passed between them in the library, it was likely he never would wish to speak with her again.

Still, once the notion had been planted, Alex found she could not entirely cast it away. Particularly not when Potter brought her the information that Stamford had asked him to tell her that she and her sisters were to dine with him as usual. That he would not tolerate, and those were his words, not Potter's, the women hiding from him by dining on trays in their rooms or in the kitchen.

Alex had no notion what it meant, but she brushed out her hair with greater care that evening before she went down to dinner, and she wore her prettiest gown. It might not be black, as was proper for mourning, and it might be a few years out of fashion, but she knew the soft blue silk flattered her. What could it hurt to let Sir Robert see what he was missing when he looked at her only as a convenient solution to his problems instead of seeing the woman she was?

Robert found himself absurdly nervous as he waited to see if Miss Barlow and her sisters would join him for dinner. He half expected she would refuse his command to appear. He also half expected she would obey, if only to prove to him that she was not a coward.

He had bungled matters badly and he knew it. He had no notion how to retrieve the situation, but he meant to try. Perhaps he had not fully explained the advantages to her? Or perhaps she wished some compliments on her person? Ladies generally did, he knew. And he still had to learn, if he could, who had actually stolen the children away from their parents and masters. Perhaps that information would satisfy Thornsby. But meanwhile, he found it oddly important to try to change Miss Barlow's mind about marriage.

Perhaps he was a fool to even try. He didn't really have to marry; that was a fiction concocted to explain his absence from London. And even without marrying Miss Barlow, there must be a way to protect her. And yet that thought did not bring him any comfort.

The sound of footsteps in the hall and the murmur of voices warned Stamford that at least two of the sisters were coming. In fact, it was all three. The younger two flanked their sister protectively, but he scarcely saw them. Instead, his eyes were fixed on Miss Barlow. From the tip of her shoes to the shimmer of her blue silk skirts to the blond curls on her head she was enchanting. Had he met her in London he might not have had the courage to ask her to dance, for he would have presumed she would look down her aristocratic nose at him. As it was, it took an effort now to bow and reach out his hand to her.

She took it, and allowed him to draw her closer. Close enough to see the pearl drops at her ears, hidden no doubt from her father or they would long since have been sold. Her eyes held something he had not seen before and did not quite understand, except that he was fairly certain his own eyes held the same.

She, however, had not lost her tongue. With a calm he wished he could match, she looked at him and said lightly, "I was surprised by your request that we join you as usual. We would understand if you changed your mind and wished to dine alone, after all."

He shook his head. "No! That is, I have never liked or become accustomed to dining alone. I should be grateful for the company."

And then she smiled. It was a tremulous smile that captured all her own uncertainty, and it touched his heart in a way that nothing else could have done. He wanted to protect her, he wanted to reassure her, he wanted to open his heart to her again, but he didn't dare. Instead, he stood there, staring down at her until Potter brought them back to the present by clearing his throat and announcing that dinner was served.

It was Miss Barlow who recovered first. "Yes, of course. Thank you, Potter. We shall come straight in. Tessa? Lisbeth?"

And then without another glance at him, she turned on her heel and led her sisters from the room. Stamford had to give himself a shake to follow.

Dinner was, he decided, almost a kind of torture. The two younger sisters suddenly wished to know all he could tell them about London. From where one might hire a house to sights to see to what the cost of food might be. Miss Barlow made more than one attempt to stem their curiosity, but it had not the least effect on the pair. Robert did his best to answer patiently, but there were far too many things he simply didn't know.

In the end, he resolved the problem in the simplest of ways. After the last of the food had been removed and the brandy bottle set before him, he dismissed the servants and then told the two younger sisters, "You may withdraw. I wish to speak to your sister alone."

He thought they would object. Rather to his surprise they did not, though Miss Barlow herself opened her mouth to speak and then closed it again. When they were alone, she said in a voice he found encouragingly mild, "Are you always this high-handed with those about you?"

"Only when I can see no other way to manage. I am sorry if I offended you or your sisters by this, but we must speak again about my offer of marriage."

She started to rise and would have fled the room if he had not clamped his hand around her wrist. She looked down at him and tried but could not hide the unhappiness in her voice as she replied, "Surely we said all that needed to be said this afternoon?"

He shook his head. "We did not say nearly enough. Please. Sit."

She hesitated and looked pointedly at his hand holding her wrist. He let it go, and after a moment she sat back down. She clasped her hands in front of her on the table. "Very well," she said, "what is it you wish to say?"

Chapter 12

Sir Robert opened his mouth several times, and each time closed it again. Each time Alex had the impression he meant to make her a pretty speech. In the end, what he said was not polished or pretty, but she could not doubt that his words came from the heart even though he could not meet her eyes and kept his own fixed on the locket at her throat.

"I want you to marry me. Not just because it would be convenient, though that was what made me think of it. But because we are alike, you and I. I know your birth is better than mine. You are accepted in ways that I can never be. But we both care about children. Children who are not titled or of gentle birth. And that is what gave me hope that perhaps, in time, you could come to care about me."

No, it was not a polished speech. But a polished speech would have left her cold, and this one most certainly did not. She reached out a hand and placed it over his. There was one more thing that needed to be said.

"I have yet to hear," she said, "whether you could ever come to care for me."

He turned his hand over and captured hers. There was a bewildered look in his eyes as he replied, "Didn't I say?"

"No."

He drew in a deep breath, and Alex held hers. Again his voice was ragged as he spoke, the words coming in halts and spurts. "I, that is when you . . .

no one ever, that is to say I always thought . . . oh, the devil with it!" he finally exclaimed. "Miss Barlow. Alexandra. I have never known what it was to care, to have someone love me or I to love them. I don't even know if I am capable of such a thing. I only know that when I hold your hand, when I look at you, when I think of all that you have done, I want to try."

And then, before he could give himself time to think or draw back, he rose to his feet, pulling Alex to hers as well. And he drew her to him until she was pressed against the length of him, her head tilted back to ask what he was about.

But she never had a chance to speak the words, for his mouth came down over hers, claiming it. It was not a gentle kiss, but Alex understood that he was not a gentle man. His arms came around her in an embrace she could not have broken if she chose. And yet she had no fear, for somehow she knew that if she truly wished for him to let her go he would.

She ought not to have liked this, to be caught up in this man's embrace and kissed until her head began to whirl. But she did. She wanted it so much that she found her arms reaching up around his neck to hold him as closely as he held her. And there was an ache within her for something more, though she could not have even begun to say what it was she wanted.

He knew though. Abruptly, he set her free and stepped several paces back. His breathing was ragged and so, she suddenly realized, was her own.

"We'd best stop," he said with an obvious effort. "Until after our wedding day. I suppose it would be wisest to post banns even though I am certain I could obtain a Special License if I wanted. But under the circumstances, I think it would be best to do things in as conventional a manner as possible."

"I . . . I have not agreed to marry you." Alex managed to find her voice enough to protest.

"Are you going to refuse me?" he asked.

She ought to do so, Alex told herself, but she could

not. Somehow she would find a way to persuade him about the children. Somehow she would make him understand. But for now, Alex could not torment him any further. Not when such an anxious look creased his brow so that she had to put her hands behind her back to keep from trying to smooth it out with her fingertips.

"N-n-no, I shall not refuse you," she stammered. "And yes, you are right that it will look better if we post banns. It will also give us time to write and let others know. You will want to invite your friends to our wedding, and I must notify my relatives, even if my father did manage to offend and alienate every last one of them."

"Which reminds me," he said a trifle grimly, "do I need to ask permission of the current Lord Henley for your hand in marriage?"

"There is no Lord Henley. My father was the last of that male line. All our relatives are of too distant a connection to inherit."

Stamford looked somewhat taken aback. "I'm surprised your father did not keep trying until he produced a son."

"Are you?" Alex did not try to conceal the coolness in her tone. "My father did not like having daughters. But if he had had a son who would one day inherit, he might have felt compelled to keep that son's interests in mind. And that would not have suited him at all. This way he could persuade himself it mattered to no one whether or not he gambled his fortune away."

He came closer and took her chin in his hand, forcing her to look at him. "I am not your father, Alexandra," he said in a clear, firm voice. "I will never serve you such a trick as that."

She did not try to argue. He meant what he said, at least for the moment. But she did not want him to make promises for their entire future that he might not always be able to keep. She said none of this aloud, of course. He would, she guessed, be offended if she did. Instead, she merely stared at him, unblinking, until he let go of her chin.

"I think perhaps," he said, "we ought to go and share with your sisters our news."

That brought Alex out of her reverie. What had she done? What had she agreed to? And what would Tessa and Lisbeth think of her betrothal?

"Afraid?" he asked, as though he could read her thoughts. Alex nodded. "Good. For so am I," he answered with a smile. "But together we will find a way to make this work."

She let him draw her hand onto his arm, and with a deep breath they went to the drawing room. That her sisters had been whispering about them was evident by the way they sprang apart with a guilty look when Alex and Sir Robert entered the room. Both of her sisters watched them with wide, curious eyes.

As though he sensed her nervousness, Stamford squeezed her hand reassuringly and said to Tessa and Lisbeth, "You may wish us happy. Your sister and I are betrothed to be married. I shall ask that the banns be read from the pulpit. As I have told her, I think it best to do things in as conventional a manner as possible."

A thought occurred to Alex. "Yes, but you have said you don't wish to do anything that will set up people's backs, and it seems to me that having a wedding so soon after my father's death must certainly do so. We, my sisters and I, ought to be in mourning for at least six months before any of us marry. Some would think a year."

He did not dismiss her concerns as foolish. He did not, however, abandon his plans either. After some moments Tessa said slowly, "Could we not say that Sir Robert was a friend of our father's? And had been for some time? That perhaps you met during your Season, but at the time he was not yet acceptable to Papa? But that on his death he commended you to

Sir Robert's care and expressed the hope that the two of you would wed as soon as possible?"

Stamford stared at her. "It sounds," he said witheringly, "like something out of a novel."

Tessa blushed fiercely, and Lisbeth could not hide her grin. Alex, however, came to her sister's rescue. "So it does," she said slowly. "But that may be its very virtue. You are concerned to be accepted by the ladies of the *ton*. Well, what would they like more than a romantic tale such as my sister has spun? And it would explain our haste. Not," she added with some haste herself, "that I am pressing for an early marriage. But if you were set on it, this would set the best light upon our doing so."

He smiled down at her in a way that warmed Alex to her very toes. "Very well," he said with what seemed almost like a twinkle in his eyes, "a romantic tale it shall be. Though not because I am afraid of the tattlemongers in the *ton*! We shall give out this Banbury tale because I do not wish you to suffer any distress."

Did he mean it? Were her feelings truly his greatest concern? She wished with all her heart that she could believe it. Instead, she covered her confusion by saying tartly, "Yes, well, we had best make certain we all tell precisely the same tale."

"Oh, no," Lisbeth objected. "You and Sir Robert must tell the same tale, of course, but it would serve far better if Tessa and I are only guessing at the details."

"And the fact that the wedding is taking place so soon after Papa's death will give us the excuse we need to keep the ceremony small so that we need not invite everyone we know. Most of them would come only to see who Alex managed to bring up to snuff anyway," Tessa said thoughtfully.

Alex shook her head. "I can see I shan't have a shred of reputation left by the time you are done," she said teasingly. "However I've no doubt you are right."

Tessa then looked Sir Robert straight in the eye
and asked, "You have not said yet what you mean to
do about the children."

He hesitated. "For the moment I shall give you
funds to see to their care."

"And after?" Alex asked. "When your friends in
the *ton* learn of their existence?"

He seemed to choose his words with care. "I will
not simply turn out the children to fend for themselves
if that is what you fear," he said. "Nor will I apologize
for caring what becomes of them. If anyone takes us
to task for it, they may chalk it up to the eccentricity
of my origins."

The bleakness in his eyes tugged at Alexandra's
heart, and this time it was she who squeezed his arm.
"Perhaps it will not be so bad," she said. "We can
make it part of the romantic tale we spin. I shall say
that it was my compassion for motherless children that
confirmed your passion for me."

He winced. It was an obvious effort, but he smiled.
"It is the truth, you know," he said seriously.

"I know."

Tessa cleared her throat. "Yes, well, now that we
have everything settled, do you think Lisbeth and I
might be excused? We really ought to go upstairs and
tuck the children in for the night. They will be delighted to know they need not creep about in the
dark anymore."

Was his smile more genuine now? It seemed to Alex
that for the first time this evening his eyes were truly
alight with pleasure as he replied, "I should like to
come up with you. I am curious to meet this brood
under my roof and to see just where they are staying."
He paused, then added, "I must admit I am relieved
to discover that the east wing is not haunted by the
ghost of a child, nor is the youngest Miss Barlow subject to fits of sleepwalking, after all. I presume those
were merely excuses to conceal the existence of the
children?"

Embarrassed nods answered his question, and it was a merry procession of four that mounted the stairs and headed into the east wing.

"Careful where you step," Alex warned him. "I was not lying when I said it has fallen into disrepair."

"I shall have to inspect it in the daylight," he said, glancing around, "and see what must be done. So long as the children are here, they must be housed in a safe and dry and warm place."

Alex ignored the twinge of worry at the way he said those words. Robert was a good man. She felt it in her heart. And once they were married, she would find the means to persuade him, if he still had any doubts, that the children belonged here with them. Even Margaret, the night she had stayed here with Alex, had said that a woman who slept with a man had a great deal of power over what he did. Well, if that were true, Alex meant to use her power to great good and resolutely, she pushed aside all doubts.

The children were in the rooms at the farthest end of the hall in the east wing. One of the maids was with them, and they were sprawled out upon the hearth. The children scrambled to their feet at the sight of Sir Robert, and one or two tried to hide behind the maid.

Alex knelt down to speak to the children. "This is Sir Robert Stamford. I know that I have told you to stay out of his sight, but that has all changed. He knows you are here now."

"Is he going to send us away?" the oldest boy asked defiantly.

"No, he has said that all of you can stay," Alex answered as soothingly as she could.

"Why?"

She hesitated, trying to find the words that would ease their fears. Stamford answered for her. He came and sat on the floor, cross-legged, beside her. He looked the eldest boy, the one who was so suspicious, straight in the eyes. Again she had the impression he was choosing his words very carefully.

"I was once very much like you," he said. "I didn't have a real home, only a place in an orphanage, and it was not, I assure you, nearly as nice as Henley Hall. I may have risen in the world, but I have never forgotten what those early years were like. I would not wish them on any child. I would never turn out a child without being certain he had a safe place to go."

There was silence when he finished, and all the adults, it seemed, held their breath to see what would happen next. First Sara toddled over and threw her arms around Sir Robert's neck. He hugged her in return. Then, as if a signal had been given, and perhaps it had, all the rest of the children shuffled closer too and took turns either hugging him or shaking his hand.

When they were done, Stamford looked at Alex, a question in his eyes. She rose to her feet. "Are you all ready for bed?" she asked.

There were nods and protests, as there always were, but when they were settled on the various cots and beds in the room, Tessa came forward and sat on the chair by the fireplace. All eyes in the room were on her, including Stamford's.

In a soft, soothing voice, she began to tell them a story about a band of children living in the woods and how they captured a dragon. By the time the story was done, the children were asleep—most of them, at any rate, and those who were not were wise enough to pretend.

As they made their way back to the main part of the house, Sir Robert drew Alex aside. "Your sister is a talented storyteller," he said.

"We think so," she agreed. "She sent one of her stories to a publisher in London, and we hope that he will wish to make it up into a book."

He nodded. Then to Lisbeth he said, "Your talent, I understand, is teaching them."

She answered almost shyly. "I like working with the children."

And then she lapsed into silence. Indeed, both Tessa and Lisbeth managed to slip away to their own rooms before the party could reach the drawing room, so that Alex found herself alone with Stamford once again.

"I like your sisters," he said.

"How convenient," she said in a dry tone.

If she had hoped to disconcert him, she failed. "Yes, isn't it?" he agreed amiably.

He paused, then came toward her, and Alex had to fight the impulse to flee. And when he took her hand in his, she had to force herself not to snatch it away.

"I hope, Alexandra, you will not find me an ogre of a husband," he said quietly. "I have been called abrupt and cold and I have very little practice courting a lady. But I will try to make you a good husband. That is the best I can promise you."

She smiled grimly. Absurdly enough, his words made her feel better. She said so aloud. "I am almost relieved to hear you say so, Sir Robert, for I have even less notion of how to be courted. I did not wish to marry, the year I went to London for a Season, and did my best to discourage every man who would have done so. I, too, have been called cold and abrupt, so perhaps we are better suited than we knew."

Whether he heard her entire speech or not, Alex could not tell. He seized on one word and repeated it even as he lifted his other hand to gently stroke the side of her cheek.

"Cold? Oh, no, Miss Barlow, the last word I should use to describe you is cold. You are fiery underneath that prim and proper exterior, and that is one of the things I like best about you."

She would have argued, should have argued, but somehow, she could not. Not when he was looking at her with such deep brown eyes, his fingers still lightly

brushing the side of her face and his other hand drawing her closer.

No, she could not claim to be cold. Not now, not
when his breath on her forehead just before he kissed
her there sent such a rush of warmth all through her.
She wore a thin silk gown, but it might have been the
warmest wool, for all she felt of the cool air in the room.
Indeed, his lips traced a trail of fire down the back of
her neck as he kissed her there and when he drew
back she could not entirely suppress a cry of dismay.

"No, Miss Barlow, not cold at all," he said. Then,
with a light flick of his finger to her cheek he told her
gently, "Go upstairs, Alexandra, and dream of me as
I shall most surely dream of you."

Confused, bewildered, lost in a sea of emotions she
could not begin to understand, Alex nodded. "Y-y-
yes, of course. G-g-goodnight, Sir Robert."

And then she turned and fled, not caring if he saw
the panic in her eyes, for she was fairly certain she
had seen an echo of that panic in his own.

Stamford stared at her retreating back. Had he
really sent her away? Of course he had, he told himself sternly, Miss Barlow was a lady. Not to be bedded
before they were bound by marriage. No matter how
much either of them wanted to anticipate their vows.

And he did. Robert could not remember feeling this
way, even about Pamela when he was betrothed to
her. But with Alexandra he knew the weeks until the
wedding would be pure torture for him. And for her,
he guessed. Who would have known, looking at her
under ordinary circumstances, that she was capable of
such passion? He had not guessed. Not until he
reached for her this evening and she had come so
willingly into his arms. Not until he had kissed her
and known, unmistakably, the depth of her response.

Some would have called it scandalous, but he found
it more promising than anything else he had yet seen
or learned about his bride-to-be. He had always as-

sumed that, if he married, it would be with great reluc-
tance. And until he spoke the words, he had not
intended to propose, but the more he thought about
his upcoming nuptials, the more he found himself an-
ticipating the event.

Chapter 13

Stamford slept through the night for the first time since arriving at Henley Hall a few days before. And he woke in a wonderfully cheerful mood. Yes, there was still Thornsby to be dealt with, but he was certain that somehow he would find a solution to that problem as well.

He frowned, however, as he realized that no one had brought up hot water for shaving. Nor had anyone opened his curtains or done any of the other things he was accustomed to waking to find done in the morning.

Even stranger was his discovery, once he was dressed and had descended to the breakfast parlor, that nothing was laid out. Not china and certainly not food. He glanced at the clock on the wall, uncertain, if he had risen earlier than he thought. But in point of fact, he had risen later than his usual time.

A sound in the hallway alerted him. He moved quickly and found the children headed for the front door. There were no other adults anywhere to be seen. At the sight of him, the children stopped and the oldest asked, "Have you seen anyone, sir?"

Robert shook his head. "I was about to go down to the kitchen to see what was going on."

"There's no one there, sir. We thought we would go outside and look," the boy told him.

"I'm hungry," Sara said, tugging at Robert's hand.

He reached down and scooped her up. "Are you?"

he asked. She nodded. He looked at the other children. "All of you? Are you hungry too?"

More nods. Robert sighed. It would have been much easier if the servants were around—or Alexandra and her sisters. He shouldn't become attached to these children. Not when he still had to tell Thornsby where they were. But there was no one else to take care of them this morning. He didn't even think about what he said next; he simply said it.

"You may as well all come with me. I shall see if I can find us something for breakfast."

"You?"

"But you're a sir!"

"Could you?"

"Why?"

This last was spoken by the oldest boy, the one who seemed wariest of him. He was answered by John, the boy Stamford had rescued.

"He can do anything!" he told the other children defiantly. "And he'll do it because he cares."

There were snorts of disbelief and rude comments. Robert found himself oddly touched by the trust and hurt by the disbelief. Was this how Miss Barlow felt? Was this why she found it so hard to even consider the notion of letting them go?

He gave the children a moment, and then he said mildly, "I don't care who believes me. I mean to make breakfast for us and whoever wishes may join me."

And then he turned on his heel and headed for the kitchen. He was still carrying Sara, and she crowed with delight at the rare treat of being held up so high. In the end, all the other children trooped after him as well.

If Robert suspected that most of them came out of curiosity or to see him fail, he did not say so or even care. What difference did it make to him? All that mattered was that these children needed his help, and he would give it to them, despite their doubts, despite knowing he ought to keep his distance. He simply could not turn his back on them, no matter what Thornsby might say.

He found eggs and bread and a few other things and soon had platters of food to set on the kitchen table around which the children had arranged themselves. His first thought was to simply set the platters down and let them help themselves. His second, wiser thought was that he had best fill their plates for them. This produced some cries of protest from the biggest ones, but the little ones were patently grateful.

Indeed, Robert had to allow, as he made a place for himself among them, that all the children were properly grateful to him for feeding them. And curious.

"How do you know how to cook?" one demanded.

"Gen'lemun doesn't cook!" another chimed in.

"I do," Robert said mildly. "Not often and not out of preference. But there was a time I was made to help out in the kitchen of the orphanage where I grew up. I was put to every task there was. There is a great deal I know how to do, even if I don't like to, or have to, do it often. Which is a good reason," he said, deciding to take advantage of the moment, "for all of you to learn every possible task you can. You never know when knowledge might prove useful."

There was some discussion of whether or not one ought to know every possible task and which tasks would be most useful to know and a discussion of which were suitable to the girls and which to the boys and at what age. Robert let the conversation swirl around him, thinking how different it was from the place where he grew up where they were supposed to eat in silence. Being children, that had been impossible, and most of them at one time or another had been punished for breaking the rules. It was, he thought, achingly nice to hear the children around him chattering completely unafraid.

But where, he wondered, were the servants? Or, if it came to that, Miss Barlow and her sisters?

*   *   *

Alex sat across the table from Margaret and sipped the tea the older woman had placed before her.

"Am I making a mistake, Margaret?" she asked her. "You know I never meant to marry. I am five-and-twenty, after all! And I always swore I would never marry just for convenience. So am I making a mistake agreeing to wed Sir Robert? Am I reacting so foolishly to a face in a locket?"

Margaret sipped her own cup of tea. She studied Alex's face for some moments before she answered. Behind her the fire dispelled some of the morning's chill, but she still pulled her shawl closer around her shoulders before she answered.

"I do not think you are marrying Stamford for convenience," Margaret said gently, "or simply because of the locket. Surely you do not believe the legend?"

Alex honestly didn't know. "Did my mother see my father's face when she looked in the locket?" she asked, needing very much to know.

Margaret hesitated again. "No," she said reluctantly. "She told me she saw another. A man her parents refused to let her marry."

Alex touched the locket at her throat, absurdly glad that it had not shown her mother Lord Henley's face. Even if it was nonsense, she did not want to think that her parents' marriage had been the answer to her mother's wishes. Still, she felt very odd, almost a little dizzy. She tried to regain her composure. Margaret was speaking again.

"I can see that your heart is touched by Stamford and that is a very different thing than choosing to marry for convenience or because one's parents say one must. Or even because you think you saw a face in a locket."

Still Alex was not satisfied. "Perhaps. And perhaps his heart is touched by mine. But he says he does not know what love is. Or whether he is even capable of feeling such an emotion."

"I see something in his face when he looks at you that tells me he is capable of love. He just needs time to discover that he can," the older woman replied. She paused and seemed to be choosing her words with care when she finally went on. "He is a good man, I think. One who has a softer heart than he wishes. He has been hurt, but not destroyed. You will heal him as he will heal you."

"I do not need healing!" Alex protested with a gasp of outrage.

She would have risen then, but Margaret reached out and clamped a hand over her wrist and forced her to sit back down. Only then did the older woman answer.

"You are hurt. You have hurt from the day your mother died. From the day you realized your father did not care what happened to you or your sisters. But I care. And now this Sir Robert Stamford cares. You are foolish if you let fear cause you to throw away the gift that has been given you."

"Margaret, you don't even like men!" Alexandra protested. "How can you tell me to trust Sir Robert?"

The older woman let go of Alex's wrist. She shook her head at the younger woman. "I dislike most gentlemen. That does not mean I cannot value the ones who are different, the ones who care or are capable of caring. He was not born to privilege and does not try to claim it as his right. He does not carry himself with the arrogance of men like your father. No, he is different, this one. Just as you are different from other women. It is your curse, or perhaps it is your blessing to be this way. You are not likely to find another so suitable mate."

Alex rose, and this time Margaret did not try to stop her. Instead, she watched as the younger woman paced about the small cottage room.

"You are right," Alex said, "I am afraid. Afraid that I shall one day find myself under my husband's thumb, as my mother did with Father."

"You did not listen," Margaret answered, "if you did not hear me say that this one was different."

Alex paced again. While she did so, Margaret poured out the dregs of Alex's teacup into the saucer and studied them. Abruptly, she sat up straighter and looked at the younger woman.

"You left him alone, this morning of all mornings?" Margaret asked with some dismay.

"Of course. What of it?" Alex asked.

The moment the words were out, however, she realized what Margaret meant. She clapped a hand over her mouth, her eyes wide with a dismay that matched the older woman's own. She turned and grabbed up her own shawl.

"I must get back to the Hall!" she said. "I thank you, Margaret, for all your good advice. But I must not leave him alone any longer!"

Margaret watched from the doorway as Alex ran along the path that led back up the hill to Henley Hall. She smiled, but it was not a pleasant smile. Nor were her thoughts entirely pleasant either. She was thinking about what the tea leaves had shown her, and she wondered just which way things would go. For Alex was at a crossroads. One way led to contentment and the things she most wished for in her heart. The other led to greater loneliness and hardship than she had ever known. Margaret could only hope that both she and Sir Robert would choose wisely.

Alex hastened along the path, hoping Sir Robert might still be asleep. Or that if he was not, that Tessa or Lisbeth had risen first and made certain all was as it should be. Surely the servants would have woken them before they left!

She'd forgotten about today. It had, after all, been years since it mattered, since anyone but her sisters had been home to know what happened. Her father would never have stood for it, and she could not guess how Sir Robert would feel. At the very least, he would

feel he ought to have been consulted, ought to have
been the one to say the tradition could or could not
continue. But no one had thought to ask him. Or if
they did, they would have decided to go ahead just to
prove they did not concede that Henley Hall was truly
his. Not until he married her.

Alexandra could hope she was wrong and that they
had acted with greater prudence, but recollecting the
silence this morning when she rose at dawn to visit
Margaret, she knew she was not. So she moved along
the path even faster. Even if Sir Robert was inclined
to sleep late, there was no guarantee, now that the
children had met him, that they could be counted
upon to play quietly enough to let him.

The moment she stepped inside the back doorway
into the passageway that led to the kitchen, Alex knew
they had been found out. She could hear Sir Robert's
voice questioning her sisters.

"How long has this *tradition* been going on? And
where the devil is your sister?"

"There is no need to curse," Alex said, stepping
into the kitchen behind him.

She drew in her breath in dismay as she realized
that not only were her sisters with Sir Robert, but so
were all the children. They were watching the adults
with wide, curious, and frightened eyes. Even those
too young to understand what was going on, understood the anger in Stamford's voice.

Alex forced her own voice to sound calm and soothing. "There is no need to frighten the children, Sir
Robert. Perhaps you and I could discuss this in the
library. Lisbeth, the children should be practicing their
letters. Tessa, I believe you have some letters to write.
Sir Robert, if there is anyone you wish to rip up at, I
am no doubt the person it ought to be. If you will
follow me, I will do my best to answer all your
questions."

There was nothing of the lover in his expression
now as he nodded curtly and indicated she should lead

the way. She did so, taking him to the library, which had, until his arrival, been her favorite room in the house.

"I ought to be with the children," she said. "But clearly you wish to know what is going on. Very well, if you will listen, I will tell you. But not if you mean to interrupt every few sentences."

It was a shrewd move, as he had been about to open his mouth and argue with her. Now, instead, he seated himself behind the desk and gestured for her to begin. Alex was almost sorry he was being so reasonable, for otherwise she might have found a way to put off answering him for a bit. As it was, she had no more excuses. And she knew just how absurd it was all going to sound.

She took a deep breath and said, "It all began five years ago. It was because of the sheep."

Chapter 14

"That much your sisters have already told me," Robert said with exasperation. "And I still do not understand. What do sheep have to do with household servants?"

"I thought you agreed not to interrupt!" Alexandra said with some asperity.

Stamford had to fight the urge to smile at her—to take her in his arms and stroke away the frown upon her lips. Instead, he crossed his arms over his chest to keep them from reaching for her, and he forced his mouth to form just one word: "Sorry."

She nodded and went on. "It began a few years ago. A neighbor's sheep were headed to market and got loose on my father's land. The servants turned out to help round them up, partly because Papa would have been furious otherwise and partly because we all knew how much the farmer needed the funds the sale of the sheep would bring him."

"Did they catch them?"

"Yes."

"Then what has that to do with no servants here today?" Robert asked, not troubling to hide his exasperation. "All I want to know is where they are today!"

She colored up with very pretty confusion. Robert had the sense that she would have bolted from the room if she could. But she didn't. Instead, though she went pale, she stood her ground and tried to answer him.

"It started, the tradition I mean, the very next year. You see, the servants had had such fun looking for the sheep and rounding them up that first year that the next year they had a morning picnic in the fields and chased one another, I am told, instead of sheep. It was foolish, I know, and most improper, and I ought to have put a stop to it at once. But they seemed to be having such fun! I knew my father didn't pay them nearly well enough or ever treat them with the least respect. It seemed to me such a little thing to indulge them in."

She paused and looked at him as though to gauge his reaction. He kept his face as impassive as he could, though he could feel a grin twitching at the corners of his mouth, and it was all he could do not to laugh outright.

"They've kept up the tradition," Alexandra explained, "of a morning picnic every year since then, including today."

"And no one thought to warn me?"

"I forgot, and the servants must have been afraid you would forbid them from doing it."

"I see. And are there any other such *traditions* that I ought to know about?" Robert asked.

She shook her head. "No."

"Think carefully," he said, leaning forward. "I can understand that there might be any number of traditions that exist only here that I should know about. And I am not even certain I should change them if I knew. But I would like to know."

That gave her pause. "I don't know," she said after several moments. "That is to say, of course we have traditions here, but I don't know what, other than the sheep hunt, is exclusive to our estate."

"Then why," Robert said gently, "don't you simply tell me everything you can think of, and if something sounds unusual to me, or I have questions, I shall stop you and ask."

She nodded and took a deep breath. "Yes. Of course. That makes a great deal of sense."

He leaned back in his chair and listened, hoping that something might give him a clue as to how all these children ended up on this estate in Alexandra's care. He could not, after all, think of any other lady who would have done what she had done, taking them all in.

It took a little while, but watching her was, he found himself thinking, scarcely the most unpleasant task in the world. When she was done, he had made a mental note of two or three oddities at Henley Hall but, in general, it seemed a rather ordinary estate. Except for the children.

Her thoughts turned to them as well. "I ought to go and see to the children," she said. "It was good of my sisters to feed them this morning, but that ought to have been my responsibility."

"Oh, your sisters didn't feed the children," Robert said, leaning back, a smile once more twitching at the corners of his mouth.

She looked aghast. "Lisbeth and Tessa didn't feed them? Why the poor things must be starving! I'd best go and fix them something to eat at once."

He was touched by her evident concern, but his voice stopped her before she even reached the door. "Your sisters did not feed them," he said softly, curious to see her reaction, "because I did."

She turned and stared at him suspiciously. "What did you feed them?" she demanded.

He told her. It was, he thought with an inward smile, amusing to see how her questions mirrored those the children had asked. And he gave her precisely the same answers. When he was done, however, it was she who surprised him. She didn't congratulate him for what he had done. She didn't seem impressed that he was capable of doing so. Instead, she looked as if she were about to cry.

"Alexandra?"

She looked at him, blinking back tears. "I know you will think it foolish of me, and it is, but I ought to have been here to take care of the children, and I am angry with myself that I was not. They were my responsibility, and I forgot."

"But they were fine," he said with some bewilderment. "The servants simply forgot to wake your sisters, so I took care of the children. They were fine."

"Of course they were fine!" she retorted. "I do not doubt, after what you have just told me, that you can and did manage perfectly well without me."

He rose to his feet and walked over to put his hands on her shoulders. "Now I understand," he said gently.

She jerked free and rounded on him. "How can you?" she demanded. "I do not understand it myself!"

But still he smiled. He shook his head and took a step closer to her. "You feel as if the children may not need you. But they do. They asked for you, you know. You are very important to them."

"Less important, perhaps, than Tessa, who tells them stories, or Lisbeth, who teaches them their letters and numbers," she said, avoiding his eyes. "And now even you."

He took her hand. "No," he said gently. "Not less. You are more important to them than Lisbeth and Tessa," he said firmly. At her startled look he went on, "Oh, we talked about you, the children and I. They adore your sisters, though not always the lessons. But it is you they look to for love. They don't call it that. They only know that you care, genuinely care about them, in a way deeper than your sisters can. And so they need you very much, no matter how many other people are about who can feed them or tell them stories or teach them their letters or numbers."

She blinked away more tears, but this time she was smiling as well. "You must think me very foolish," she said.

"Don't be absurd!" he retorted. "I think you are a

woman with a generous heart. And while I despise
your father for gambling away his inheritance and
making you and your sisters penniless, I am very
grateful that his doing so gave me the chance to find
you."

She blushed then, very becomingly, he thought,
though again she seemed embarrassed by her reaction.
Well, he understood that. It seemed sometimes to
Robert that he had spent his entire life being embarrassed by his emotions. So now, afraid to overwhelm
her even more, he kissed Alexandra lightly on the lips,
then instantly drew back before she could object.

"I think," he said in a careless tone, "that perhaps
we ought to go and see the vicar and arrange for the
banns to be read from the pulpit as soon as possible."

He half expected an objection, but she made none.
Instead, she nodded, a trifle shyly, he thought, and
said, "Give me a few minutes to change from my old
gown into something nicer and I shall be ready."

"Of course."

He watched her go, and then sank into the nearest
chair. For the first time since he had seen her this
morning, it occurred to Robert to wonder where she
had been and with whom. Had she been out with the
servants hunting imaginary sheep? Somehow he didn't
think it likely. She had too practical a turn of mind
for such things. Besides, to have the daughter of the
family about would have spoiled half the fun for the
servants. No, she had been somewhere else, and Robert found himself wondering where.

As she changed into her best black dress, Alex
found herself pondering Sir Robert's reaction. Her father would have been furious if he had found himself
in these circumstances. He had had no patience with
Mama's wish to look after their tenants or their tenants' children, much less those of strangers. And he
would have been furious that the servants felt they
had the right to a morning to themselves.

But Robert was not her father, Alex reminded herself firmly as she put on her bonnet. Margaret had adamantly said so, just this morning. This was more proof that she was right.

Thank heavens Sir Robert had not asked where she had been. How could she have explained she had gone to consult Margaret about him? But then, she realized as she took a deep breath and drew on her gloves, there would have been no need to say so anyway. She could merely have said that Margaret had told her to come and have her head looked at, and it would have been the truth, albeit not all of it.

Downstairs she found Sir Robert in the foyer, waiting for her, but without showing the least trace of impatience. He looked at her and frowned. "I shall be glad when you put aside your mourning," he said. "Black, even in silk, does nothing to flatter you and grants your father far more respect than he deserves."

Alex let him hand her into the carriage before she replied. Only when they were settled and on their way did she speak. She did not try to hide the impatience she felt as she said, "That may be so, Sir Robert, but we are going to see the vicar, and I assure you he will expect just such a show of grief and respect on my part. If I were to ignore convention, I would only set up his back, and we might very well find that he refused to post the banns!"

"Oh, I make no doubt you are right," he replied with a smile, taking not the least offense at the sharpness of her tongue. "I only meant that when the time comes, I shall take great delight in dressing you as you deserve—in silks and satins and velvets, all in the richest of colors. Your eyes will sparkle even more than they do now, and the bloom in your cheeks will have every man's eyes upon you."

Alex turned to look at him incredulously. "And do you think I wish for that?" she demanded.

He smiled disarmingly, and there was laughter in his voice when he answered. "No. But grant me suffi-

cient male pride to wish for it on my own behalf. I
shall enjoy walking into a ballroom in London and
having every man there envy me because you are
my wife."

Alex blushed, furious at herself for doing so. She
detested such missishness! But she could no more stop
herself from coloring up than she could stop the stam-
mer that occasionally afflicted her speech. Particularly,
it seemed, when she was with Sir Robert.

It was nonsense, of course, everything he said—as
though she belonged in richly colored silks and satins
and velvets. And yet she could not deny a certain
wistfulness at the thought that someday it might be
so. Nor could she deny how pleasing it was to hear
him say that someday other men would envy him,
even if she thought he must be teasing her or simply
trying to set her at ease, or some such thing. Because
even if that were so, it was still more kindness than
any other man had ever shown her.

All too soon they drew up at the vicarage. Interested eyes peered from the windows as Sir Robert
handed her down from the carriage. The vicar had a
large family, and every one of his offspring was no
doubt reporting in loud voices that Miss Barlow from
up at the Hall had come to call and had the new
master of the Hall in tow.

As if to confirm her suspicions, the front door of
the vicarage opened before Sir Robert could even lift
his hand to knock. And it was the vicar himself who
answered, a grim look in his eyes as he welcomed
them.

Alex's heart sank as she saw that the vicar meant
to be difficult. He was going to ask, she suddenly realized, why she and her sisters remained under Stamford's roof when there was no woman there to act
as chaperone.

She could only hope that the news that he was going
to be asked to perform a wedding ceremony would
placate the worst of his suspicions and disapproval.

But since she had known him from her earliest years and in all that time he had never wavered from his strict principles, she had the unfortunate feeling he was not going to make this easy for them.

Alex was correct. The vicar showed them into the small room that served as his library and invited them to be seated. His words were cordial enough, but the moment the door was safely closed behind them, he came to stand before the pair and said, "All right now, have you come to tell me how much longer the pair of you intend to continue to live in sin?"

Chapter 15

"Live in sin?" Robert echoed incredulously. He half rose to his feet, and only Alexandra's hand on his arm stopped him.

"Are you not living under the same roof with Miss Barlow and her sisters without a chaperone?" the vicar demanded.

"Miss Barlow is my housekeeper," Robert said through gritted teeth. "When I arrived and discovered the impecunious circumstances in which she and her sisters found themselves, propriety and the need for a chaperone were the furthest thoughts from my mind. Are you suggesting I ought to have turned them out?"

"You might have removed to an inn," the vicar suggested evenly, "though I will allow that since the property was yours, that would have been expecting a great deal of you."

"I am glad you concede the point," Robert said with obvious irony.

The vicar, however, was not done. "You might also have sent the girls to me," he persisted.

"They would not have gone," Robert said, without hesitation. Then, abruptly realizing he had perhaps spoken a trifle too hastily, he turned to Alexandra and asked, "Would you have gone?"

She shook her head. "No." To the vicar she added, "My sisters and I are past the age of having to worry about such things. In any event, I had accepted the responsibility of housekeeper in exchange for permission to remain in my family home, and surely you could not have wished for me to abandon my responsibilities?''

The vicar hesitated. He removed his spectacles and polished them with his handkerchief. It was evident he was suffering from a great deal of agitation and indignation. Nonetheless, he made an effort to restrain himself. When he spoke, his voice was as stern as ever, but he tried to choose words that would not reveal the depths of his emotion. It was evident to Robert that he was a man who prided himself on his self-control.

"I see. You make it sound very plausible. But you, Miss Barlow, and Sir Robert are living under the same roof without a chaperone. And no amount of explanation can change that fact. What I wish to know is how much longer is this going to continue?''

Robert smiled and steepled his fingers. He crossed one knee over the other and leaned back in his chair, enjoying the sight of the vicar's rising anger at his apparent lack of concern. But because he could feel Alexandra's distress, he did not wait very long before he answered the man.

"Only as long as it takes for the banns to be read on successive Sundays, and then you may perform the wedding that will make everything right and proper.''

The vicar gaped at him and then at Alexandra. Abruptly, he closed his mouth and began to grin. "Why didn't you tell me so at once?'' he demanded. "This, of course, changes everything! Not, mind you, that I approve of what came before, but we shall say no more on that head! A wedding. Well, well, what delightful news to bring. That is''—he broke off to look at Alexandra and ask—"if you are certain this is what you wish? If it is not, you and your sisters are very welcome to come and stay with my family until you can find another solution to your situation.''

Robert held his breath as he waited for her answer. He thought he knew what it would be, but there was a part of him that was achingly uncertain.

She rose to her feet and kissed the clergyman on
his cheek. "You are very sweet to offer, sir, but I
know only too well how full your home already is.
Besides, I do wish to marry Sir Robert. He has shown
my sisters and me nothing but kindness and respect,
and those are, as you yourself have said to me upon
more than one occasion, excellent foundations for a
marriage."

Now Robert rose and put an arm around her waist.
"Will you marry us, then?" he asked the vicar. "Are
your concerns sufficiently satisfied?"

The vicar reached out to shake his free hand, carefully ignoring the other that rested on Alexandra's
waist. "They are, Sir Robert. And may I say how
happy I am that you have come here—that it is a man
with as much sensibility as you possess who now owns
the estate?"

Robert grimaced. "Yes, well, I cannot think it hard
to improve upon Lord Henley. Not after what I have
heard to his discredit since I came here. I would not
speak ill of the dead, but I find it hard to forgive any
man for so thoroughly abandoning his daughters and
recklessly disregarding all thoughts of their future and
how to provide for them."

"Excellent sentiments," the vicar agreed. "I am glad
to hear you speak with such heartfelt warmth. When
we heard that someone had been so cruel as to win
Henley Hall from his lordship in a game of cards, well,
we thought the man must be entirely heartless."

A pang of regret shot through Robert, as it had so
many times since he learned of Henley's suicide. "I
did not mean to let matters go so far. But he was
drunk and insisted that we keep playing. He insisted
that I accept his vouchers for the estate or he would
have tried to call me out. But I never meant to keep
it," he said, forcing out the words. "In a week or so
I should have returned the vouchers to his lordship
on condition that he retire to his estate and never
gamble in London again. It will always haunt me that

he killed himself before I had the chance to make my intentions known to him."

"He would not have thanked you," Alexandra said quietly, her eyes wide, her expression strained. "Papa would have thrown the vouchers back at you rather than ever agree to give up his beloved gaming. Heaven and the vicar knows how often my sisters and I begged him to do so."

He squeezed her waist reassuringly. "You need never fear that I shall follow in his footsteps. If you wish, I shall make you just such a promise now."

She smiled at him, and it was all Robert could do not to bend forward to kiss her. The vicar cleared his throat, ostentatiously recalling them to where they were and who was with them.

The man had a suspicious glint in his own eyes, however, as he said, "Your words do you credit, Sir Robert, and I am very happy to hear you speak them. Very well, I shall read the banns beginning next Sunday. And send them to be read in your parish as well, Sir Robert, if you will give me the direction. The two of you will find yourselves wed before you even know what is happening! It will be my great pleasure to see it happen and speak the words that will make you man and wife."

He paused and turned to Alexandra. "But until then," he said sternly to her, "I wish you to ask Margaret, who lives in the woods, to come and stay at Henley Hall. It may only be a matter of a few weeks and some will say the damage is already done, but you know, even if Sir Robert does not, what a difference it will make in how the pair of you are treated after the wedding."

"You consider Margaret to be a suitable chaperone?" Alexandra asked, echoing the incredulity Robert felt.

The vicar sighed. "I will not deny that I would prefer someone more conventional. But she is convenient to hand, and despite her living in the woods, she was once a lady. Or so I understand. In any event, I cannot see how you will find anyone else even remotely suitable without a lengthy delay, and I really must insist you have someone today."

"Very well," Alexandra replied.

Robert wanted to object. He thought it absurd. But he could see that Alexandra agreed with the vicar. And surely she must know better about such things than he could. He had not been raised, as she was, from the cradle to know what was considered right and proper and necessary.

Robert sighed. He truly thought he had learned to know the rules, but perhaps there were some he had overlooked. Certainly it had never occurred to him there would be a problem with staying under the same roof as the Barlow sisters. Not when Alexandra was his housekeeper. Would there always be such gaps in his knowledge, in his understanding of *tonnish* ways? Still, apparently she was not altogether satisfied with the vicar's suggestion either.

"What if Margaret will not come?" Alexandra was asking the vicar.

He looked at her and polished his spectacles again. "Leave that to me," he said. "I believe I may be able to persuade her to come and stay with you. In fact, I shall send a note to her as soon as you leave that will explain the situation and why I believe she should come and stay with you. With your permission, of course."

Alexandra looked at Robert, as if asking *his* permission, and he found himself oddly touched. He smiled at her and said, "I've no objection. Fill the house with chaperones if you like! And after Margaret took such good care of you when you were hurt, I can scarcely object to her presence under my roof in any event."

The tremulous smile she bestowed on him lifted Robert's heart in the most alarming way. He had never known he could feel like this, and he found it a trifle frightening. The vicar, however, seemed pleased.

"My dear children, I am glad to see such affection between you. But I must insist, however, that you speak with my wife, Miss Barlow. She will be wanting to hear the news directly from you, you know. And I, well, I should like a chance to speak with Sir Robert alone."

That seemed to give Alexandra pause. But Robert had no such qualms. He gave her a tiny push toward the library door. "I shall be fine," he said teasingly. "If I do not join you within half an hour, you may come back and rescue me. That is, sir, if you think half an hour will be sufficient time for you to satisfy yourself as to my character?" he added, looking at the vicar.

"Quite sufficient."

It was a warning as much as it was an agreement, but neither Robert nor Alexandra were inclined to cavil at it. Instead, Alexandra smiled and left the room. Robert sat down again and pretended to an ease he did not entirely feel.

The vicar sat behind his desk, and Robert was reminded of his school days and the times he had been summoned to face the headmaster. He felt something of the same sensation now, and he guessed the questions would be no easier to answer than they had been then. Though he had, perhaps, a trifle clearer conscience at the moment, he thought with a wry smile.

The vicar seemed to understand precisely the direction of his thoughts. He also smiled and began to talk. His voice was stern at first, but the longer they conversed, the more the two men discovered how much they liked each other.

"Which is fortunate," the vicar conceded as he opened the library door some time later and gestured to Stamford to precede him, "if I am to live on your bounty. Henley Hall funds my parish, and therefore you are going to be forced to listen to my sermons every week."

With a grin that came naturally now, Robert retorted, "That, sir, I promise you I shall scarcely find a hardship!"

The vicar wagged a finger at him, "Now, now, do not speak with such certainty until you have spent a Sunday or two sitting on our hard benches." He paused. "I must be serious a moment, Sir Robert, and thank you. I have worried for some time what would become of the Barlow girls and could hit upon no satisfactory solution. I am glad to see you here, glad to see the kind of man you are, and glad to know that Miss Barlow will find a kind husband in you."

And then, before Robert could even begin to find the words to answer him, the vicar threw open the doors to the parlor, where his wife and Alexandra and several of the vicar's children were all engaged in animated conversation—conversation that came to a dead halt at the sight of him in the parlor doorway, conversation that abruptly started up again, hastily, as everyone tried to pretend they hadn't been staring quite so avidly at his person.

Perversely, that made Sir Robert feel better, for it made him feel how human they all were. So he was able to enter the parlor with a light step, greet the vicar's wife with ease, and even play for a bit with some of the younger children. None of which did him any harm in either the vicar's or his wife's estimation.

Still, it could not be denied that he felt a marked degree of relief when he was finally able to escape with Alexandra from the vicarage. At least, he told himself, the worst part of the day was over.

Chapter 16

By the time Alex and Sir Robert returned to the house, the servants were back and all but humming with good spirits. Her sisters had the children well in hand, and it promised to be a wonderful day. Or so Alex thought.

They had not been home an hour, however, when she chanced to look out a window and saw a handsome carriage coming up the drive. "Who could that be?" she wondered aloud.

Robert, who had heard the noise and also come to look out the window, smiled as he saw the crest on the carriage. "If I am not mistaken," he said, "it is my friend Lord Ransley. And no doubt his wife as well since he is not driving his curricle. You will like them, I am sure."

By now the carriage had drawn to a halt, and liveried footmen were beginning to deposit baggage on the top steps to the house. A gentleman and lady descended from the carriage, and they were obviously discussing something with great animation.

Alexandra was too stunned to speak. Guests? A lord and lady? To be sure, they had entertained any number of titled guests while Papa was alive. But not when the house was in such disarray.

"I must arrange for bedchambers to be prepared," she murmured.

"And find your sisters. Tell them to hide the children," Robert said. "I shall go down and greet our guests. It is a good thing the vicar sent for Margaret

to come and stay. After what he said today, I've no
doubt Lord and Lady Ransley would be just as
shocked as he was to discover we have been living
here without a chaperone."

And then he was gone. Alex felt a twinge of dismay
that Robert wished her to hide the children. But she
couldn't really feel surprised. He had already told her
how much his standing in the *ton* meant to him. And
she understood that a lord and lady were unlikely to
approve of her eccentricity in taking them in. However
disappointed she might feel, for as long as Lord and
Lady Ransley were guests in this house, Alex must
find a way to keep the children hidden.

There was no time to waste, she realized. The servants were, fortunately, still in excellent spirits. They
had no worries about guests. Indeed, Cook was
pleased to have a chance to show off her skill.

"For depend upon it, Sir Robert won't be wanting
plain fare," she told Alex. "Not with a lord and lady
here to visit he won't. Ah, I mind me of the days we
did this all the time. When you were a little one, Miss
Barlow. Don't you fret—we'll have it all well in
hand here."

A maid agreed to run to Margaret with the message
that there were guests here from London and she was
needed as chaperone even sooner than expected. Alex
could only hope that the older woman's quick wits
would fill in the rest and know what was needed.

Another maid was set to airing two bedrooms for
Lord and Lady Ransley, side by side, with orders to
put fresh sheets upon the beds. Then Alex raced up
the back stairs and into the east wing, her sisters'
voices drawing her swiftly to the right rooms.

The children stared at her wide-eyed as she tried to
catch her breath. She explained matters as quickly and
quietly as she could. Without protest, the children
gathered up their things and headed farther down the
hallway to the rooms at the end. They might not have

understood the reasons for Alex's distress, but they understood and cared enough to do as she said.

Finally, Alex spoke to her sisters. "I've got to go downstairs and greet Sir Robert's guests. I'm not certain how he means to present us, or if he does. I'll send word to you when I know."

Tessa and Lisbeth nodded. "Don't worry about us—we'll see to the children," Lisbeth said.

"Sir Robert had better not introduce you as the housekeeper," Tessa said fiercely. "Not when he has said he means to marry you!"

Alex smiled and tried to reassure her sister. "I have no notion what he intends. He is no doubt as stunned as we are, for I'll swear he had no expectation of guests. We shall simply have to see how things go on. But you may as well know the vicar has already agreed to read the banns this Sunday, and he has insisted that Margaret come up to the house to act as chaperone."

"That," Tessa said, rolling her eyes, "should be most interesting. I wonder what Sir Robert's London guests will make of her?"

All three sisters smiled at the thought. It was impossible not to, for a less worldly woman than Margaret could scarcely be imagined. And yet neither could they, even for a moment, imagine her daunted by the highest ranking of lords and ladies. Yes, it should prove most interesting to see how Margaret would deal with this lord and lady and how they would deal with her.

Still, it was time to go downstairs. Robert must be wondering what had become of her and the guests, particularly Lady Ransley, who would be expecting the housekeeper to come and show her to her room.

Sir Robert, however, had done an excellent job of delaying their guests, and even as she descended the staircase, she could hear their voices coming from the foyer below.

". . . to rescue you from boredom."

"And to warn you that Prinny is still upset. He is adamant that you are not to show your face in London until you've got a wife in tow."

"That, my dear friends, is already taken care of."

Alex clung to the banister at the sound of Robert's voice speaking so calmly. There was not the least trace of the affection he had shown her earlier. Instead, she would have said his voice was completely devoid of any emotion when he responded to their exclamations of astonishment and demands to be told who the woman was.

"Henley left a daughter. To be precise, he left three. The eldest will do. She will be quite sufficient to satisfy Prinny's anger. The banns are to be read beginning this Sunday, so, if you are willing to return in a few weeks, you can even see me wed."

"Henley's daughter?" Lord Ransley sounded taken aback. "That loose fish? But aren't the girls all on the shelf? Past their last prayers?"

"I want to meet Henley's daughter now," Lady Ransley replied, a grim note to her voice.

Now Stamford laughed. "Why?" he asked.

"So I can see what sort of harpy she is," Lady Ransley told him roundly.

"Harpy?"

Well, at least Robert sounded genuinely taken aback by the notion, Alex thought with grim satisfaction.

"Well, she must be one," Lady Ransley explained, "to have talked you into marriage within a few days of your arrival here. Or did she trick you into a compromising situation so that you have to marry her?"

Alex swallowed hard. She'd known there might be talk, so why was she surprised? She had to fight the impulse to run upstairs and hide. Somehow, some way, she would have to make herself go down the stairs. But perhaps not quite yet. Not until she heard more of what Stamford's guests had to say. And Robert.

She could almost hear the smile in his voice as he told the tale they had agreed upon.

"Really, Lady Ransley, you are letting your imagination run away with you. I fear the story is far more mundane. I met Miss Barlow years ago. But I was not, in Lord Henley's eyes, an eligible suitor. And his antipathy then was, in fact, the reason I wagered against him in what turned out to be his last game. For revenge, though I find it quite hollow now. But when Prinny banished me from London, I knew I had to come and see Alexandra—to discover if she was still the same woman I admired years before."

"And was she?" Lady Ransley demanded.

"What the devil is she doing here? If you won Henley's estate, why isn't she living somewhere else?" Lord Ransley demanded, his mind patently focused on the practical details of the story.

Robert took his time in answering. He responded to Lord Ransley's objections first. "Henley's daughters had nowhere else to go. The eldest, Miss Barlow, asked to stay on as housekeeper, and I accepted."

"You made her your housekeeper?" Lady Ransley asked in shocked tones.

Again Alex could hear the smile in Robert's voice as he replied, "Well, yes, but I knew it would not likely be for long. I always suspected, you see, that once we saw each other again, Miss Barlow and I would discover our sentiments had not altered. And I was right. So while she may have briefly been my housekeeper, she is about to become my wife. Aren't you, Alexandra?" he asked, betraying that he knew of her presence on the stairs.

She had no alternative but to descend the rest of the way and smile as she took the hand he reached out to her. He drew her to his side and put his arm around her waist. Even if it were simply for show, it felt right, somehow, to have it there. And neither Lord nor Lady Ransley appeared shocked to see the intimate gesture.

But the two guests were not yet won over. Lord and Lady Ransley surveyed her from head to toe, and it was not an altogether friendly inspection. Finally, Lord Ransley bowed and said, "I am delighted to meet you, Miss Barlow. I had no notion Stamford was so sly."

Lady Ransley was equally reserved. Her smile was perfunctory, but not as hostile as it might have been. "He has just been telling us his news. I presume you are also in alt over your impending nuptials?"

Alex looked up at Robert. She had no notion how wistful her expression was, how much emotion her eyes betrayed. And when he smiled at her, she had no notion that a tremulous smile danced on the corners of her lips to match his.

"Yes," she said at last, "I am in alt. I had not thought to wed or, if I did, that I would be so fortunate as to be able to wed Sir Robert after all."

Lady Ransley gave a tiny crow of delight. "So it truly is a love match? My deepest apologies, Miss Barlow, for thinking otherwise. I am delighted. If ever there was someone who deserved happiness, it is Stamford. Now come and tell me everything!"

Alex looked at Robert, this time with alarm. He pulled her tighter and said to Lady Ransley, "Later. For now you will have to be content with both of us showing you to your room, for I will not let Alexandra leave my side. Dearest, into which room have you placed our guests?"

"I-I placed them in adjoining rooms. The ones opposite yours," Alex answered. The Ransleys looked at each other with some dismay. "Do couples not wish for separate bedrooms?" she asked, a trifle bewildered. "My parents always did."

Neither Lord nor Lady Ransley could quite bring themselves to answer, and Robert did so for them. "To be sure," he said in soothing tones, "a great many couples prefer it so. But not Lord and Lady Ransley. For that matter, I do not think," he added, "that after our marriage, I will wish for us to have separate bed-rooms. Will you?"

Alex colored up to the roots of her hair. She could not even begin to think how to answer such a sally nor where to look. It was patently impossible to meet either Lord or Lady Ransley's gaze.

Lady Ransley took pity on her. "That is quite enough, Stamford!" she scolded him. "You are putting poor Miss Barlow to the blush. If this is how you treat her, have a care she does not bolt before the ceremony!"

"Oh, I've no fear of that," he answered lazily.

When Alex looked at him indignantly, she saw the laughter in his eyes and was disarmed by it. She could not, however, resist teasing him. "Lady Ransley is right," she said. "You'd best treat me properly or I may refuse to go through with the ceremony."

What he would have answered in return Alex never did find out, for at that moment a familiar voice said from the back of the foyer, "That is quite enough! Sir Robert, I will thank you to unhand my niece until after the wedding."

Niece? Alex and Stamford looked at each other with matching confusion, which they hastily hid from Lord and Lady Ransley, who had turned to greet the new arrival. Fortunately, Margaret had her wits about her. She came forward dressed in a more elegant gown than any Alex had ever seen her wear before, and she moved with a poise and elegance of character that seemed equally strange.

"I am Miss Winsham, Miss Barlow's aunt. Her mother was my sister, and I am, in some sort, her chaperone. That is to say, if she needed one, which, at her age, I should think she does not," Margaret said.

As the Ransleys greeted her, Robert and Alex ex-changed more confused glances. In the end, all they could do was pretend to accept the situation as though it were nothing in the least new or unusual.

"Shall I take you upstairs to your room?" the older

woman asked Lord and Lady Ransley. "You may wish to change or rest for a few minutes before you come back downstairs. Meanwhile, my niece will make certain that a cold collation is laid out in the parlor for us in an hour. Unless you would like something now?"

If they were a trifle dazed, Alex could not blame them, for she felt that way herself. Both Lord and Lady Ransley disclaimed any need for immediate refreshments. And they quite docilely followed Margaret up the stairs.

The moment they were out of sight, Robert dragged Alex into the library and shut the door and demanded an explanation. She couldn't blame him, for she would have liked one herself.

Chapter 17

"You didn't tell me that Margaret was your aunt!" Robert exclaimed, feeling as if he had wandered into Bedlam. "What the devil is she doing living out in the woods?"

"She isn't my aunt," Alexandra replied, obviously trying to keep her voice low so that they could not be overheard. "I don't know who she is. She has lived in the woods for as long as I can remember. All I know is that she is interested in healing and that she and my mother were friends."

"So she was lying?"

"I don't know. I must presume so, but until I can ask her, I have no notion why she said such a thing!"

For the first time Robert calmed enough to realize that Alexandra was even more upset and bewildered than he was. In as soothing a tone as he could manage, he said, "Well, since she has claimed kinship, we, none of us, dare deny it. Not with Lord and Lady Ransley here. You had best warn your sisters. And when it is possible, ask Margaret what she meant by saying such a thing. But for the moment, at least it provides you with an apparently suitable chaperone. I must admit she looks very different than she did the last time I saw her in this house. Whoever Margaret is, it would seem that the vicar was right when he said she was once a lady."

His soothing tone and matter-of-fact words had their effect. Alexandra began to relax. He could see the tension leave her shoulders. She even managed a smile.

"I have never in all the years I have known Margaret ever seen her in a dress so fine! But I think you must be right that she was once a lady. And you are also right that I must warn my sisters not to deny her as our aunt."

She paused and seemed to want to go on, but could not bring herself to do so. "What is it?" Robert prompted her.

Alexandra raised her clear green eyes to his. "These people, Lord and Lady Ransley. Are they really friends of yours? Or people who would do you harm if they could?"

He grinned. He could not help himself. It warmed him to his very toes that she should care, that she should feel such concern on his behalf.

"Friends, they are most definitely friends. Don't you remember? I told you so when we looked out the window and saw their carriage. I have known Ransley since we both arrived in boarding school. And we have stood at each other's back through more fights than I care to remember. I once admired his wife before she was his wife, but happily stepped out of the way once it became evident how much they cared for each other. You will find very little pretense in them, nor snobbery either."

"But it would still be as well to hide the children, I presume?" Alexandra asked.

"Children? You have children?" a light voice called from the doorway. "You are a widow then? I must have misunderstood. I thought Sir Robert called you Miss Barlow. But no matter, I should love to meet your dear little children! How many have you?"

Robert saw Alexandra go very straight and very rigid at the first sound of Lady Ransley's trilling voice, and she only became more tense as the words continued. He tried desperately to think of a way to handle matters that would not result in disaster. Lord and

Lady Ransley were dear friends of his, but he could not tell them about the mission Thornsby had sent him on. Nor could he bring himself to simply pretend that he meant to raise the children as his own.

Lady Ransley looked from one to the other. She was perceptive enough, Robert knew, to guess that something was very wrong. A moment later she proved him right.

The smile fell away and concern touched her eyes as she said quietly, "Clearly I should not have interrupted you. But the door was partway ajar, and I could hear you in the hallway. I only meant to put you at ease, Miss, that is Mrs. . . . er, Barlow, about the children."

Now Alexandra spoke, and it was with some constraint. "You were correct the first time, Lady Ransley. It is Miss Barlow. And yes, the children in some sense are mine. Children I have taken in. I care for them deeply, but I doubt very much you would wish to have their company inflicted upon you. Now I pray you will excuse me. I must see that all is well above stairs. My sisters are with the children. You will have the chance to meet them, my sisters that is, at dinner."

And then she fled the room before anyone could speak, before Robert could even try to reassure her. She would not meet his eyes or she would have seen the silent message of support he meant to give her.

When they were alone, Robert turned to Lady Ransley. She looked most contrite.

"I am sorry, Sir Robert. I meant no harm."

How could he explain that he was angry not with her but with himself? For letting her overhear, for caring so much what she thought, for wondering more whether it would affect her opinion of him than how it might affect the children themselves.

In any event, Robert could not stay angry with Lady Ransley. Not when she and her husband had always been his greatest supporters. Besides, he would need her help when he brought Alexandra to London and introduced her to the *ton*. And he would need her support if the *ton* ever learned about the children.

"Do you truly wish to help?" he asked.

"Yes, of course!" she answered swiftly. "You know I would not wish to cause you pain. Or your bride, either. Tell me how I can make amends."

"Let me begin by telling you the truth," he said.

"That would be a good start," she shot back.

He gave her a look of reproof, and she sat down, but her expression was completely unrepentant. Robert sighed. This was not going to be easy. But at least it was practice telling the story to someone who would listen with a desire to understand, a desire to be sympathetic.

"You know my background," he said, for neither he nor Lord Ransley had ever hidden it from her. She nodded, and he went on. "Well, then, you will understand that when I discovered Miss Barlow and her sisters had rescued some children, I was pleased rather than otherwise."

"Yes, of course, but why does she house them here? Why hasn't she sent them to an orphanage?" Lady Ransley asked, bewildered.

Robert hesitated. While he had never hidden his background from her, neither had he ever told her the dark side of those early years. He hated that he hesitated now to tell her the truth, that he could not bring himself to remind her even more of how different he was from most of the *ton*. She, he was certain, had never known the sort of hell that had been his home for too many years of his life.

In the end Robert simply said, "Because Miss Barlow has a generous heart."

"A generous heart, yes, but not the funds to back it up," Lady Ransley protested. "She has been caring for them on your generosity, and I'll be bound she did not ask your permission beforehand."

"I do not object, I assure you," Robert said with

quiet firmness, wishing it were the truth. "It is one of the things that made me fall in love with her."

He half feared she would seize on the word love and taunt him with it. That, at least, would have served to divert her from the other matter. But she did not. She continued to pursue the question of the children.

"But what do you mean to do with them, with the children, after you are married?" Lady Ransley demanded. "You cannot continue to keep them in the house with you."

"Why not?" he asked, curious to see what she would say.

She gaped at him. She opened, then closed her mouth several times before she finally managed to answer.

"Because . . . because it isn't done!" she said. When he didn't answer, she went on, "Surely not all orphanages are horrible. And you must think of yourself. You have worked very hard to achieve success and acceptance. I know because my husband has told me a little of the difficulties you have overcome. To keep such children about you will remind the *ton* of your background and cost you all that you have worked for. I do not ask you to abandon them, but only to face reality. And to ask yourself if what you propose is even best for them, for I do not think it is."

And to that Robert had no answer. He could not tell her about Thornsby and the people clamoring for the return of the children they had so badly mistreated. He could not tell her his own confusion over how best to handle matters. As for raising the children with Alexandra, Lady Ransley had merely put into words his own fears. So instead, he did not speak to the issue of the children, but rather of Alexandra.

"I hope you will be kind to Miss Barlow," he said. "Whatever you may think, she is going to be my wife. And I think she will make me happy. Certainly I shall try to make her happy. It will ease her way consider-

ably if you will show her kindness and help her find
her way when we come to London after the wedding."

Lady Ransley wanted to object. Robert could see it
in her face. But she bore too much kindness for him
to do so, and in the end she sighed and said, "Very
well. For your sake I shall do my best to set Miss
Barlow at ease and to help her if I can. For your
sake. Because you care for her. And because however
foolish I think her to take in these children, it is evident she cares very much for you."

That startled Robert. He wanted to ask Lady Ransley how she could know that Alexandra cared for
him. But just then Lord Ransley pushed open the library door in search of his wife, and she rose to go
with him. Robert said all that was proper, but when
he was once more alone, he looked around the library,
the room that had most come to feel like home, and
he wondered what he was going to do.

He hated that in the end it might come to a choice
between the welfare of the children and the position
in society that he had fought so long and so hard to
obtain. He was not proud of himself that he was not
sure which would win.

Upstairs, Alex found her sisters and warned them,
not only that Margaret was here and claiming to be
their aunt, but that Lady Ransley now knew about
the children.

"Does that mean we need no longer hide them?"
Tessa asked.

"I don't know. Sir Robert and I had no chance to
discuss the matter," Alex replied. "For now they must
be kept out of sight, but at least we need not hide
their existence entirely. Which might have been impossible in any event."

"Is Margaret really our aunt?" Lisbeth asked, her
thoughts on the other matter.

"I don't know," Alex said, repeating the words she
had just spoken about the children. "I have not had

the chance to talk with her yet. But since she has claimed that kinship, we dare not contradict her in front of Lord and Lady Ransley. But neither do I like to lie, and if it is a lie, sooner or later someone is bound to say so. I had best go and try to find Margaret and ask her what possessed her to say such a thing!"

"Yes, go and do so," Tessa urged her older sister. "And don't worry. We shall manage the children. One of the maids will be here to watch them soon so that Lisbeth and I may change and join you and your guests. As for dinner, Cook appears to be in alt and is, she said, planning something very special."

Alex squeezed her sister's hand in thanks, then headed back toward the main portion of the house. She had to find Margaret and talk with her before any more tales were told. She had to find out the truth.

As if of their own accord, her fingers stole up to grasp the locket that hung from the chain around her neck. It was absurd to think that Margaret could really be her aunt, and yet, if she were, it would explain why Mama had left her locket for Alex in her care. And it would explain why, before she died, she had spent so much time in Margaret's cottage, often taking her eldest daughter with her.

But if it were true, how and why had Margaret ended up living in the woods? Why had she never married and had a family of her own, for she patently loved children? It was a mystery either way, one that Alex wished resolved as quickly as possible.

She found Margaret inspecting the linen closet. At the sound of Alex's footsteps, the older woman closed the closet door and turned to greet the younger one. "You've done an excellent job of mending some of these sheets," she said briskly. "Before I leave, I shall show you a stitch or two that will do the trick even better."

"Margaret—"

Alex cut herself off before she even began. This was not, she realized, a conversation she wished to hold in a hallway. Instead, she said, "Why don't we go to your room to talk, *Aunt* Margaret?"

The older woman grinned at the way Alex stressed the word that appeared to connect them. She merely nodded, however, and led the way to a chamber that was rarely used. Indeed, Alex could not remember the room ever being used for guests. For all her childhood she remembered it locked, and no one had seemed to know where to find the key.

But it was apparent that at some point the room had been used because when the door was closed behind them, Margaret looked around the room and turned to Alex.

"This," she said, "was the room I always used when I came to stay with your mother and father. I left my gowns here when I chose to move into the cottage, and it was understood that my things would be kept for me here. You were still very young then and would scarcely be able to remember me before I did so."

"You truly *are* my aunt?" Alex asked.

Margaret smiled at her, and it was as though years fell away. She no longer seemed the ancient crone Alex had always thought her to be, but a woman a good many years younger than her mother would have been, had she lived.

"I am indeed your aunt," Margaret agreed, "your mother's younger sister, but I prefer my cottage to the nonsense of society. I had to promise your father, however, that I would never admit to the connection if he was to let me live in his woods to grow and study plants. But I don't believe that promise matters anymore. Not when you have need of a chaperone. Instead, I'll promise that so long as I play that role, I will not speak of my life in the cottage."

Dazed, Alex could only nod. After a moment, however, she gathered her wits enough to smile and say, "I have an aunt! I am delighted to discover that it is you, Margaret!"

"No, you are not," the older woman said tartly,

"but it is excellent manners for you to say so. Still, you must become accustomed to referring to me as Aunt Margaret and Miss Winsham. One wouldn't wish Lord or Lady Ransley to think we were eccentric. Now come—we ought to go downstairs and see to the comfort of our guests."

"Wait—there is one more thing," Alex said. "The children. Lady Ransley overheard Sir Robert talking with me, and she knows there are children here."

"And?" Margaret prompted.

"I don't know what we should do about them. I don't know what more Sir Robert told her after I left the room."

"Then I suggest," Margaret said tartly, "that you go and ask him."

Chapter 18

But Alex had no chance to ask Sir Robert anything. With one domestic crisis after another, due to the arrival of their unexpected guests, she did not have a chance to speak to him until dinner.

The three sisters came down together, dressed in gray. Margaret wore purple silk. The dress was many years out of fashion, but she wore it with such dignity that no one would have dared to tell her so. The four stood together, as though to give one another courage and support.

But Lady Ransley greeted Alex warmly. "You need not stand on ceremony with me, Miss Barlow," she said. "You have made Sir Robert happy, and that is enough for me to know we shall be friends."

Lord Ransley came to stand behind his wife and rest a hand on her shoulder. "I, too, wish to thank you. Stamford looks far happier, far more content, than he ever did in London. I vow the Prince of Wales will be most astonished when he sees him and even more astonished when he sees you, Miss Barlow."

"The Prince of Wales is bound to command an appearance from the pair of you the moment he learns of your marriage," Lady Ransley added cheerfully. "Then Stamford can return to London and the life he loves."

"He loves London?" Alex echoed slowly.

"My dear woman, did he not tell you?" Lord Ransley asked with an amiable grin. "The man lives for the excitement there. I cannot imagine him content anywhere else!"

"I see," Alex said faintly.

And she did. Indeed, it was not that she had never known, but rather that she had allowed herself to forget that inconvenient truth. It was, after all, why he was so eager to marry her. Oh, he had said all the pretty words to make her feel wanted, but patently it was the need to return to London that mattered most. She had simply not wished to believe it.

The room seemed too close, too warm, and Alex had to put a hand on a chair to keep from feeling faint. She liked Sir Robert. More than that, she'd lost her heart to him. Or rather, to the man she thought he was. But listening to Lord and Lady Ransley talk about Stamford was a reminder of how little she knew about him.

And then he was there, standing before her, concern in his eyes. Despite her doubts and that it made no sense to her, Alex suddenly felt as if things would be well after all. There was a sense of safety in his nearness she could not explain. And a sense of calm.

"Are you all right, Alexandra?" he asked, and she could not doubt his concern.

"I . . . yes, of course."

"We have been telling tales on you!" Lady Ransley told Stamford playfully. "Perhaps we have even shocked her, and you will once again find yourself without a fiancée."

Alex forced herself to laugh. She would not betray herself or Robert to these people. "How absurd!" she said with a lightness she did not feel.

But there must have been something in her voice that betrayed her, for Robert looked at her now with searching eyes. And Alex found she wanted and needed his reassurance.

In a bright, cheerful voice she said, "Lady Ransley has been telling us that the Prince of Wales is bound to command an appearance from us the moment he hears we are married."

"No doubt he will," Robert agreed. "But don't worry, I am certain he will find you charming."

He smiled at her reassuringly, and she smiled at him in return. But still Alex worried. How important was this to him? As though he sensed her turmoil, Robert took her hand and tucked it under his elbow. It was meant to hearten her, but she felt more confused than ever.

"Careful!" Lady Ransley warned playfully. "You will shock the *ton* if you carry on such displays of affection in public in London!"

"As we did?" her husband teased.

It was Margaret who rescued Alex and Robert. "Tell me, how did the pair of you meet?" she asked Lord and Lady Ransley.

As Robert's friends turned to answer Margaret, he was able to draw Alex away to the other end of the room. She was grateful for that kindness and for his efforts to put her at ease.

"Please do not let them trouble you," he said. "I meant it when I said the Prince of Wales would find you charming."

"Is that so very important to you?" she asked.

He looked down at her face, his eyes searching hers. "Not more important than your comfort," he replied carefully.

She wished she could believe him. Perhaps it was even true. But what if it was not? Abruptly, she realized he was speaking again.

"By the by, what did you discover about Margaret?" he asked, glancing over to where she stood talking to his friends.

"That she is, indeed, my mother's younger sister," Alex replied, pleased to see that her voice sounded calmer than she felt. "I still do not know why she moved into the woods, but she is indeed my aunt."

He shook his head. "Incredible! Well, the devil will be in it if anyone in London learns of her eccentricities!"

Alex found it hard to speak. "Does it matter so very much what people in London think?" she asked.

He looked at her, and once again she had the sense that he was choosing his words very carefully. "I had thought to bring your sisters to London at some point. To give them the sort of Season they deserve. Another chance, perhaps to find husbands. It will be harder for them, and for us, if the *ton* knows of Margaret's eccentricities."

Perhaps he saw that she meant to argue, for he went on, "We cannot entirely ignore the opinions of others, Alexandra. No matter how much we might wish we could do so. Whether we like it or not, those opinions may sometimes determine the choices we must make, the things we must do."

"Surely what matters most is that we do what we believe is right?" Alex argued.

"If one is content to always be on the outside looking in, then perhaps that is so," Robert replied. "But if one is part of a greater whole, then one must not entirely ignore the opinions of others."

"I see. And that is why you do not wish to keep the children with us?" she asked in a low voice that would not carry to the others. "For fear of what others will say? And that matters more to you than that you were once a child in need of someone to care about you?"

He looked at her impatiently, a hint of grimness about his eyes and mouth. "No one in London is ever likely to let me forget who I am and where I came from," he said, "regardless of what we do about the children."

"Then why do you wish to go back to London?" she demanded. "Why not stay here, where you will not have to face such prejudice?"

He hesitated, and she felt that he was holding something back. When he spoke, Alex did not doubt that Robert meant what he said, but she had the oddest feeling that it was only part of the truth.

"Long ago I made myself a vow that one day they,

the *ton,* would have to accept me," he said in a low voice pregnant with unspoken emotion. I made a vow that one day they would have to acknowledge who I have become. And with you at my side, they will."

She wanted to ask him if that was all she was to him—a means to an end. But Potter announced that dinner was served, and it was time to smile and rejoin the others and indulge in only the lightest of chatter over dinner.

Cook had indeed outdone herself. Alexandra could not help wondering where she had obtained the necessary ingredients for the succession of dishes placed before them. She had not thought they could manage half the number.

"You must bring your chef to London when you come," Lord Ransley told Stamford. "He is far better than the one you have there now."

"She," Alex said, stressing the word, "would be most unhappy to leave here."

Lord Ransley blinked. "Surely you do not coddle your servants, Miss Barlow?" he said. "What the devil do her wishes have to say to the matter?"

"A great deal," Robert said with a disarming smile. "You are tasting her work at its best. I assure you, you would not wish to taste it at its worst, as I did when she first resented my coming here."

For a moment Lord Ransley stared at his friend, then laughed. "You are quite right," he allowed. "One does not wish to land in disgrace with one's cook. Oh, very well, you shall simply have to retire here often and invite your very best of friends to join you."

The moment had passed, but Alex still felt the sting of Lord Ransley's disregard of Cook's feelings. Perhaps something of this showed on her face, for Lady Ransley leaned over and said quietly, "Men do not understand the delicate matter of obtaining and keeping excellent servants. A woman would never have said such a foolish thing. Indeed, I cannot tell you the

lengths to which I have gone in order to make certain
my staff is happy!''

Alex smiled then, disarmed by the woman's wish to
reassure her. But as the chatter droned on, she found
herself thinking that this was what it would be like in
London. She would feel out of place and people would
say things that made no sense to her. She had not
liked her one Season. Would it be any better when
Robert took her there now?

London, it seemed, was on everyone's thoughts. ''I
still think you ought to present Miss Barlow to the
ton as your fiancée before you present her as your
wife,'' Lord Ransley said to Stamford. ''Why not take
her to London now?''

''No!'' Alexandra protested. ''That is, I cannot see
the need.''

The answer was instinctive. The children needed
her, and she could not leave them. More than that,
she needed time to accustom herself to the notion that
she must go to London at all. But she could scarcely
say any of that aloud. As it was, Lord and Lady Ransley exchanged speaking looks.

It was Margaret who once again came to Alex's
rescue. In a calm voice she said, ''I think it would be
better if Sir Robert presented the *ton* with a *fait ac-
compli*. And the Prince of Wales. More than that,
surely the *ton* would wonder at my niece traveling to
London with Sir Robert on her own, and I cannot
leave my other two nieces to go with her. And we are
needed here.''

No one quite felt capable of asking Margaret why
they were needed at the estate. The force of her words
was felt, however, by at least one person. Lady Ransley tapped her chin thoughtfully.

''Miss Winsham has a point,'' she said with a sigh.
''It is a pity, but don't worry, Miss Barlow, Lord Ransley and I will stay and keep you company until after
the wedding.''

Alex looked at Robert in alarm. They meant to stay

until after the wedding? That would mean weeks with these strangers in the house. She could not possibly keep the children out of sight for that long! Though perhaps, since Lady Ransley knew about them already, it would not be necessary?

Lord Ransley said, "You could always be married by special license, of course. Then you would not need to wait."

"I have no wish to offend anyone by omitting to have the banns read," Robert answered with a frown.

"Under the circumstances, I think you might argue that the need to present yourself to the Prince of Wales, without delay and with a bride in hand, would justify such a step," Lord Ransley said thoughtfully. "And there is the circumstance of Lord Henley's recent death. Indeed, one could also argue that it would be more appropriate to be married by license in a private ceremony than to hold a larger wedding after posting banns."

Robert looked at Alex, and she wished she could know what he was thinking. Did he want her to make the decision? If so, she did not know what to answer. She had known him such a short time. Would she be making a dreadful mistake to agree? After all, wasn't the point of having banns read to give the couple time to think through their decision? And yet, she knew somehow that her answer would not change, no matter how many weeks they waited.

"Perhaps Sir Robert and I could discuss the matter privately after dinner?" she suggested at last.

There were nods of approval, and to Alex's relief Lord and Lady Ransley no longer pursued the matter. Still, it seemed an eternity until the meal was over.

But in the end, the ladies rose from the table and Stamford rose as well. He came to take Alex's hand, and he said, so that all the others could hear, "I think, my dear, that perhaps it is time for us to talk."

Alex took a deep breath. "Yes, I think perhaps it is," she agreed.

Chapter 19

They went to the library, and for once Robert did not go behind the desk, but rather drew Alexandra to sit in a chair near the empty fireplace. He took the chair opposite hers so that he was only a foot or two away and so that he could see her face clearly.

"I am sorry for the enthusiasm of my friends," he said.

"They clearly care very much for your welfare," Alexandra managed to reply.

"As I care for theirs. But right now I am concerned about your wishes. I do not think you wish to be married by special license."

She shook her head. "No. This is all so sudden as it is, our betrothal, I mean. I . . . I need the weeks it will take to read the banns to become accustomed to the notion of being your wife. I had not thought ever to marry, you see, and it is not precisely easy to think of doing so, even now."

Robert nodded and tried to reassure her. "Of course I understand! I must confess that I need some time as well to become accustomed to the notion of being a husband. This is very new and sudden for the both of us."

She was silent a moment, and then she said carefully, as though not wishing to offend him, "Do your friends really mean to stay here until we can be married?"

He hesitated. "I need to leave in the morning, and I will be gone for a week or two. I should like to ask

Lord and Lady Ransley to stay so that you are not left entirely alone."

"You have to go?"

The stricken look in her eyes made Robert feel better in a way he could not explain, even though he also felt a twinge of guilt over why he had to go.

"I promise I will be back in time for the wedding," he assured her. "But there are some things I must do."

"What?"

That was the difficult part. He could not tell her. He could not explain to Alexandra that he had to see the people who had said their children were stolen. He had, after all, only her word that the children had been misused. And even if it was true, Thornsby was not going to be pleased at what he meant to do. He had to speak to these people before he spoke to Thornsby.

Aloud, however, Robert turned the tables on Alexandra. "Will you miss me, as I shall miss you?" he teased. He lifted her hand and kissed the palm. "I promise to return as quickly as I can."

She blushed adorably, and he found himself wanting to take her in his arms. But this was not the time for such things. For now he had to keep his wits about him and say the things he needed to say.

"I see you do not mean to tell me where you are going and why," she said, refusing to be distracted. "Very well. Then tell me—after you return and we are married, do you really mean for us to go to London?"

"Yes."

That gave her pause. "For how long?"

He hesitated, thinking of all that would need to be done about the children, and the way he wanted to show her about. "At least a month or so," Robert replied.

"And if I do not wish to go to London?" Alexandra asked.

Again he hesitated. He had no wish to ride roughshod over her, and yet this was too important. He had to take her to London. Still he hoped to persuade her to go.

"It is very important to me," he said coaxingly.

Alexandra stared at the empty fireplace. "I hated London when I was there," she said, her voice coming as if from a long way away. "I don't want to go back."

"It is necessary," he persisted. "I have never made a secret of my ambitions. And perhaps, when you are seeing it with me, you will like London."

"Will I? Perhaps." She looked at him then. "But Robert, perhaps you ought not to marry me, after all. I am not likely to be the wife you wish, not if you truly prefer London to here."

How could he explain? How could he make her see what it was he felt? In the end, he settled, as always, for a part of the truth.

"No matter how you feel about London," he said, making his voice as earnest as he could, "I still want you for my wife, Alexandra. Yes, I hope that when you see it with me, you will come to love London, though of course we would also spend time here. But even if I knew for certain that you would hate London, I would still say that we should marry."

Robert paused and drew in a deep breath. "The vicar will read the banns while I am away, and we may both become accustomed to the changes that marriage will bring to our lives. Please believe that we are making the right choice, both of us."

"And whether I wish it or not, after we are married, we are going to London."

"Yes."

"I see." Her face was pale and her voice not entirely steady as she went on. "I think perhaps we have said enough for tonight. I had best go and join my aunt and sisters and our guests."

He had hurt her. He could see it in her face, and he didn't even understand why. What was so terrible about going to London? he wondered.

And Robert hurt, too. He had not known, until this

moment, how much he wanted her to want to be by his side always. How much he wanted her to understand what going to London meant to him. How much he wanted her to want to go there for his sake.

For all his angry vows over the years, Robert had not truly known, until he proposed to Alexandra and she accepted, how much it meant to him to perhaps finally be welcome in the circles she moved in. And having tasted that dream, he could not let it go. Somehow the need to resolve the problem of the children with Thornsby had gotten all tangled up with the wish to be accepted by the *ton*. And at the moment, Robert could not even say which was stronger.

He tried to tell himself such misunderstandings, between himself and Alexandra, were to be expected. They had known each other, after all, for less than a week. And perhaps he ought to be grateful that he was discovering now, and not after the wedding, how stubborn she could be. He ought to be grateful at the possibility she might cry off. Why the devil should he want to be leg-shackled anyway? But sensible or not, there was no mistaking the dark feelings in his soul at the thought of losing Alexandra.

That was how Ransley found him, sitting in the chair behind the desk and staring into the empty fireplace, as Alexandra had done such a short time before.

"Stamford? Are you all right? Are you and Miss Barlow to be married by special license?"

"No. I must leave here tomorrow. I've some business to conduct elsewhere, and I shall have to see to it before the wedding."

Ransley blinked. He stared at his friend, and Robert was well aware that his distress must be visible and he ought to say something more. But because he could not speak to anyone, not even his friend, about the dilemma of the children and Thornsby, he pretended instead to be thinking only of his presumed marriage.

"Miss Barlow and I are still going to be married,

but after the banns are read, just as we originally planned. And then we shall go to London, and I shall be able to inform Prinny of my wedding. Perhaps then he will finally acquit me of intending to mount his mistress!" he said lightly, as though it was a jest.

"Will he?" Ransley asked, not troubling to hide his doubts. "You were remarkably attentive to her."

"I *was* attentive," Robert growled, playing the role he had been assigned as though it were true, "because Prinny asked me to see to her comfort, nothing more! We have been through this before. Do you honestly believe I should prefer a woman older than myself to the charms of Miss Barlow? Prinny's tastes may run in that direction but I assure you mine do not."

"Nor mine," Ransley agreed. "Very well, if you mean to leave tomorrow, Lady Ransley and I shall return to London. It would not do to impose upon Miss Barlow's hospitality if you are not here."

"Actually," Robert said slowly, "I was rather hoping you would stay."

"What?"

Robert hesitated. How to explain without telling Ransley about this particular assignment for Thornsby? He chose his words very carefully.

"It may be foolish on my part, but I have reason to think there might be those who carry a grudge against Miss Barlow. I do not like to leave her and her sisters alone here while I am gone," Robert said.

Ransley eyed him shrewdly. "Lord Henley made a number of enemies," he agreed. "And you think that some might be angry enough to wish to take revenge against his daughters? Seems dashed unlikely to me, but not impossible, I suppose. And I do see that you might want your friends to plead your case for you while you are away."

Robert grinned. "You know me far too well!" he said, seizing upon the excuse gratefully.

"Very well, we'll stay," Ransley said. "But mind you, when you do go to London, I want to be there to see Prinny's face when you tell him that you are leg-shackled! I'll wager he thought you could not find any lady who would agree to such a match and that he knew you had too much pride to settle for less."

"In short, you think Prinny expected to banish me from London forever?" Robert asked with some surprise. "Why should he wish to do that?"

Lord Ransley eyed his friend shrewdly. "Do you really not understand? You have done him more than one signal favor—rescued him from more than one scrape. Do you truly think a man of his temperament can bear to be reminded of that every time he sees your face? This incident with his mistress was but an excuse. If not that, he would have found another. Go back to London, Stamford, and by all means see Prinny and tell him your news. But give up the notion of being part of his circle any longer."

Robert was silent for a long time. It had not occurred to him that Prinny's command had been anything more than too great an enthusiasm for the role Thornsby had asked him to play. But his friend's words made sense. Perhaps Ransley was right and Prinny had hoped to banish him from London for good.

He was silent for such a long time that Ransley came and placed a hand upon his shoulder. Robert looked at his friend and made himself smile.

"You are an excellent advisor. And I know your words are more sensible than anyone else would have the wit to tell me. It is hard, however, to accept that I have lost that entrée to the *ton*."

Lord Ransley shook his head. "You've lost nothing important. Your bride will bring you enough respectability to make you welcome. Lord Henley may have been a selfish old fool, but his line was a long and most respectable one, until he came along. Marrying his daughter will go a long way to making you acceptable. Particularly once it is known you are otherwise in Prinny's black books. There are those who will take you up just to spite him. And don't you dare refuse their invitations!"

In spite of himself, Robert laughed. "You know me very well. I hope you may be right. For my bride's sake, if not my own."

"Yes, well, only time can prove me right or wrong. For now, perhaps we should join the ladies."

That was the last thing Robert wished to do. He had plans to make if he were leaving in the morning and a letter to write to Thornsby. But he could not be so rude as to abandon his guests simply because he had work to do. Not when he was supposed to be nothing more than a careless rake. Besides, with Margaret in the house, he thought it best to make certain he knew just what she might be saying to Lady Ransley.

Sir Robert looked completely unconcerned at their impending separation, Alex thought, as he entered the room—as though the notion did not distress him in the least. Did he truly have business that he must deal with? Or was it that he could not wait to be rid of her company? She touched the locket at her throat for comfort.

Alex looked over at Lady Ransley who was listening to Margaret with great fascination, and she felt a pang of guilt. She really ought to be paying attention. Margaret no doubt meant well and at one time must often have spent evenings like this. But it must have been years since she did so, and Alex could not help but feel anxious as to what the older woman might say to their guests.

But it was Robert who had the greatest claim upon her attention. He was explaining that he would be going away on business and leaving in the morning.

Then she heard Lord Ransley say that he and his wife meant to remain until the wedding. She'd forgotten that Robert had said he would ask him to stay. And she had forgotten, in the shock of hearing that he was going away, to ask why. Lady Ransley looked distinctly taken aback, and Alex knew she would have to do her best to set the poor woman at ease.

Margaret, she noticed, was staring at Robert in a way that made Alex distinctly nervous. But she neither said nor did anything to give offense. Not, at any rate, while Alex was watching!

Robert returned to the library when the others went up to bed. He had maps to consult, a journey to plan, and a letter to write to Thornsby.

It was the latter that was the most difficult and, by the time he was done, his mood was very, very foul. He had not precisely lied to the man, but close enough that Thornsby might think so. And there was no getting around the fact that, one way or another, he was going to have to disappoint and distress either Thornsby or Alexandra about the children.

He also knew he ought to have someone stay and keep an eye on the children. He couldn't precisely have said why he thought it necessary, only that he did. The question was who should he have stay? Which of his servants would be both discreet and yet show sufficient initiative to be willing to undertake the task of watching the household without quite knowing what it was he was watching for?

Unbidden, the footman Dunford came to mind. He had been hovering about the kitchen the first day, listening. And yet he had not said a word to Robert about what he overheard. That argued both discretion and initiative. The question was, what else did it say about the man? There was only one way to find out.

Ten minutes later, Dunford stood in front of Stamford's desk. His expression was wary but intelligent. Yes, Robert thought, this man might do.

"How do you feel about being here?" he asked.

"Sir?" the man asked, clearly taken aback.

"How do you feel about being here? Would you mind if I asked you to stay behind and help to look after the children while the rest of your fellow servants came with me?"

"Depends on where you'll be going," Dunford answered cautiously.

"I'll be going to a lot of places, driving hard for probably two weeks straight or more. I may or may not stop in London, but I shan't stay. So, would you rather come with me or stay here?" Robert asked.

It didn't take Dunford long to make up his mind. "Stay here!"

"Why?"

Again the man looked surprised. But when he saw that Robert was serious, he replied bluntly, "I don't much like this place. Prefer Lunnon, I do. But I'd rather be here than jaunting all over, clinging to the outside of a coach for two weeks or more, half the time in the rain, no doubt."

Robert smiled, pleased rather than offended by the man's honesty. "Good," he said. "Then I want you to stay here and spend your days helping out with the children."

"What am I to do with them?" Dunford asked, unable to hide his dismay.

"Let's call in the maid who usually looks after them and ask her how you may be of help," Robert replied.

He sent someone to fetch the woman. While they waited, he continued to talk with Dunford. "I also want you to keep your wits about you," he said. "I shall be curious to know what you see and overhear while I am gone."

The man nodded slowly, and Robert had the impression that he understood. Which was fortunate because the maid arrived sooner than Robert had expected, cutting short the time he might have spent explaining things to the footman.

"Sir, you wished to speak with me?" the woman asked, coming into the room and making a curtsey to Stamford.

"Yes. Betsy, isn't it?" She nodded. "I should like

you to meet my man Dunford. I am leaving him here to help with the children while I am gone for the next few weeks. I should like you to guide him and explain what sort of help he can give you."

If Dunford had been taken aback, Betsy was even more so. She did not trouble to hide her dislike of the notion. "Him?" she demanded with a sniff. "What use is a footman with children? Is he going to help bathe them? Comb their hair? Wash their faces? Will he tuck them in at night or play with them? Or do you mean for the sight of his face to frighten them into obedience?"

Dunford choked back an outraged roar. Instead, when he answered her, his voice was cold with disdain. "I am quite certain I can undertake to do any of those tasks, however little you think so. I were raised with eight brothers and sisters. I think I know a little about taking care of children!"

She sniffed again. "If you say so. And if Sir Robert insists, then I suppose I shall have to accept your help."

Robert had to hide the grin he was quite sure neither of them would appreciate. "Good," he said in as matter-of-fact a voice as he could manage. "I shall expect you to work together while I am gone. I leave in the morning, but I shall come by to see the children before I do, and I expect to see both of you there, helping each other with them."

They both grumbled, but neither dared disagree. They did, however, seem relieved when he dismissed them. Well, that was one problem solved, Robert told himself. Now if only the rest would go smoothly as well.

Chapter 20

Alex found Sir Robert with the children the next morning. There was also a strange footman, one of Robert's servants brought from London, she guessed. Though why he should be helping Betsy she could not fathom.

Robert scarcely noticed her. He was watching as Tessa told the children a story, and Sara, the youngest one, had climbed into his lap. The bleak look in his eyes tugged at Alex's heart, and she wondered who he was going to miss more, her or the children.

"Your carriage is waiting out front," she told him quietly.

Startled, Robert set down Sara, rose to his feet, and colored up as if embarrassed to be caught there. "I, er . . . thank you." To the children he said, "Good-bye. I shall be back in a few weeks. Mind you pay attention to Miss Barlow—to all the Miss Barlows. And to Betsy and Dunford. He is here to help look after you."

Alex waited for him, and as they walked back down the deserted hallway, she asked, "Why is your man Dunford with the children?"

He hesitated, and as she so often did, she had the sense he was choosing how much to tell her. "I thought it would help take some of the burden off your shoulders if you had a man here to help with the children. Particularly with the boys it is just as well to have a man nearby."

She could not precisely argue with that, for more

than once they had caught the older boys engaged in mischief. So she nodded and said, "Lord and Lady Ransley are downstairs waiting to say good-bye to you." She paused and looked at him. "I have the impression they are not altogether pleased to be staying, and I cannot say that I blame them. There is little here they can possibly find entertaining."

He started to speak then seemed to change his mind. His voice was light and careless as he answered her, but he would not meet her eyes.

"No, no, it is me they are displeased with. They arrive one day and I depart the next. It is not very hospitable of me, I fear."

But Alex would not let him play such games with her. She stopped him by putting a hand on his arm. Her own voice was low but firm as she asked, "Why are you going away? And why now? You say it is business, but what business? Why did it so suddenly arise when your friends appeared? And why did you ask them to stay here while you are gone?"

He hesitated, and this time when he answered her he did meet her eyes, and Alex had the sense that this time he was, perhaps, telling her the truth.

"It was not entirely sudden, my needing to go," Robert said, a hint of sadness in his face. "I had hoped to be able to put it off, but when Lord and Lady Ransley arrived, I realized that I cannot do so forever. And though I will miss you, it is best I take care of things before our wedding."

"Why?" Alex asked, searching his face for an answer.

He smiled that wistful smile of his and said, a teasing note to his voice, "Why so that I can devote myself entirely to you after we are married, of course. And I want Lord and Lady Ransley to stay here and come to know you so that they will come to like you as much as I do. That would be a great help when we go to London."

"I see. Nothing could be more natural," Alex

agreed dryly. "At least that is what you wish me to believe and that is all you mean to tell me. Very well, I shall not tease you. But I shall miss you, I think."

He paused and seemed to catch his breath, as she caught hers at the look in his eyes. His voice was barely a whisper as he leaned forward and said, "Here, then, is something to remember me by."

And he bent his head toward hers. She had time to escape if she wished, but Alex had no wish to escape. Instead, she found herself swaying toward him, wanting the touch of his lips on hers, wanting his arms to come around her and pull her into his embrace. It was not right; it was not proper. But those words had little meaning now when she felt as though she was about to lose someone very precious to her.

Nor did he disappoint her. He kissed her brow and then the tip of her nose and then her mouth. He was gentle, and the kiss felt like a promise—a promise that he would be back, a promise that they could be happy together, a promise that she could trust him.

And then he let her go, his voice as sober as his expression. "Have faith in me, Alex, no matter what happens."

Before she could ask him what he meant, he set off toward the stairway at a brisk pace, and Alex had to hurry to catch up. And then they were face-to-face with Lord and Lady Ransley and she could do nothing but stand back and watch them jest with Robert and help to see him off. But his words echoed in her mind as she watched him climb into his coach and pull away from Henley Hall. What on earth could he have meant by asking her to have faith in him, no matter what?

The three of them, Alex and Lord and Lady Ransley, stood on the top step watching until Robert's coach was out of sight. Then Lady Ransley linked her arm with Alex's and said, "Come, let us go and have a cup of soothing tea. Sir Robert will be back before you know it, and Ransley and I shall be dancing at your wedding."

And because there was nothing else to be done, Alex let herself be persuaded.

She didn't expect to like having the Ransleys stay at Henley Hall. But she found Lady Ransley, or Helen as she asked Alex to call her, a comforting companion. Lady Ransley was not so much older than Alex, and she still remembered how it felt to fall in love.

"For it was a love match with Lord Ransley and myself, you know," Helen explained one morning when they were alone at breakfast. "I thought Papa would have apoplexy when I told him I wasn't going to marry the man he had chosen for me. Lord Ransley was even more surprised when I told him he was going to offer for me."

Alex choked on her morning tea. "I should think so!" she managed to gasp.

But Helen was not in the least offended. She continued to eat her food, oblivious to the gaping stares of both Alex and the servants. "It wasn't very proper of me, of course, but I didn't care. I knew he would need a push. You are fortunate that Sir Robert needed no such help," she told Alex.

"I . . . I suppose I am."

Helen looked at her, eyes twinkling. "Now that I have utterly sunk myself beneath reproach in your eyes, let us change the subject. Tell me, what gown do you mean to wear for your wedding?"

"There was a dress of my mother's," Alex explained hesitantly. "Tessa and Lisbeth and I have taken it apart and salvaged what material we can. There should be quite enough to make a gown for me. Mama was bigger than I am and the styles a bit more full back then. You may see us working on it later if you wish."

Lady Ransley frowned. "You do not have a seamstress in the village to help?"

Alex looked down at her plate, then tilted up her chin in unconscious defiance. "Even if we had the funds," she said, "there is no one I would rather trust than my sisters and myself with something so important as this."

"I see."

But what it was Helen saw she did not say. Instead, she turned the talk to other matters, then rose from the table as Tessa and Lisbeth came into the breakfast parlor. Alex was not sorry to see her go. Alone with her sisters she could ask about the children and help to plan their day.

It was several hours later that Alex saw Helen again. She rapped on the parlor door and exclaimed with delight as she saw Tessa and Lisbeth pinning the gown into its new shape on Alex as Margaret supervised.

"Beautiful!" Lady Ransley exclaimed. "Clearly the three of you are notable needlewomen." She paused then added, "You will not, however, have time or material or funds, I would guess, to outfit Alexandra properly before she must leave for London."

"We shall manage," Lisbeth said stoutly.

"I have no doubt you shall try," Lady Ransley replied. "But I doubt any of you have even seen the latest fashions, much less have the means to copy them."

"What do you suggest, then?" Alex asked, tilting up her chin in the same unconscious gesture of defiance as at the breakfast table that morning. "Or do you mean to simply disparage our efforts?"

But Helen did not answer at once. She merely smiled and circled Alex. She tapped her chin thoughtfully.

"I believe," she said at last, "that I have a solution for you. Subject to your approval, of course," she added hastily at the look of mutiny upon their faces.

Tessa lifted a skeptical eyebrow, Lisbeth snorted her disbelief, and Margaret asked dryly, "And your solution would be what?"

"Alexandra is," Lady Ransley said slowly, "much

of a size with me. And her coloring is not so different that she cannot wear the same colors. I do believe I've a number of gowns in my wardrobe she could wear and they would flatter her. I've spent the morning sorting through what I brought with me, and I should like to make her a present of them."

"Why should you do that for my sister?" Tessa asked, not troubling to hide her suspicions.

Lady Ransley smiled. "I could tell you that it would be out of friendship for Sir Robert. And that would be true. But," she added with a mischievous smile, "it is also true that if I give your sister a generous portion of my wardrobe, my husband will have to allow me to replace it with new gowns when we return to London and that, my dears, I assure you would be no hardship to me!"

The Barlow sisters could not help laughing. Even Margaret permitted herself a small smile. It was clear that Lady Ransley meant what she said. And that it would be of mutual benefit to her and to Alex to agree. It was also clear to Alex that Helen would have made just such an offer even if it had been a sacrifice to her. And she was grateful.

But Lady Ransley would not permit the sisters to thank her. "No, no," she said airily. "You are doing me the favor. Now what I should like to know is when you, Miss Winsham, are going to come to London with the younger Miss Barlow sisters."

"Never!"

Margaret muttered this more to herself than to Lady Ransley, but Helen heard her. "Nonsense! Surely they would like to see London?"

Tessa answered first. "I should like to go," she said. "I should like to see if I could find someone to publish my stories."

"I see. And what about you?" Lady Ransley asked Lisbeth.

"I should like to see London again," the youngest

Miss Barlow admitted wistfully. "And this time I would like to go to balls and parties and the theater."

"There! You see? You must bring them to London. I am certain Sir Robert would be happy to have all of you stay with him," Lady Ransley said triumphantly.

"Oh, to be sure," Margaret replied tartly. "I can think of nothing Sir Robert would find more delightful than to have my nieces and myself descend upon him in London!"

Helen and Margaret exchanged a few more pointed barbs, but Alex did not listen. Her thoughts were on Robert, wondering where he was and what had been so urgent that he must leave her before their wedding. Didn't he want to get to know her better? Didn't he want to know how she felt, what she knew, how they would deal together?

Was it that he was so certain the match was a good one, or was it that he simply didn't care? Or perhaps he had begun to have second thoughts and hoped she would cry off if he was gone long enough? Alex realized that she didn't have the slightest notion which possibility was true, and she found that a very lowering reflection.

As foolish as it seemed, she had lost her heart to a man she knew less than a week, and Alex could not imagine the rest of her life without him. She would have left the other women and gone up to her room to curl up in a chair and think about Sir Robert, except that the whole purpose of their gathering here was to work on the dress for her wedding. She could scarcely expect them to do so without her. And so, with a tiny voice within asking if she were ever truly going to wear the dress, Alex forced herself to join in once again on the discussion of just how they should fit the dress to her and what changes ought to be made in their original design.

Chapter 21

More than two weeks later, Robert's thoughts were on Alexandra as his coach rattled along the main road into London from the north. He stared out of the window and wondered what she was doing. More than that, he wondered what she would think if she knew what *he* was doing.

How many men had he seen? Too many. Some had been persuaded to drop their search for the missing children when he asked certain pointed questions of them. Others had threatened to strike him. One man he had knocked down.

None of them understood the wrong they were doing. Each felt fully justified in mistreating the children they had paid for. No wonder the children had run away! If there were any surprise, it was that more children had not done so.

He no longer wondered that Margaret and Alex had taken the children in. But he still did not know what he was going to do about them, what he was going to say to Thornsby. He had never had an assignment quite like this one. He had never before wavered in what he knew to be his duty. Indeed, he had taken pride in helping to enforce the law. And now? Now he was torn between duty on the one hand and his heart on the other. And he didn't know what he was going to do.

So he stared out the window as they entered London and continued to wonder what Alexandra was doing right that moment, and how soon he would be able to see her again.

He sighed as the coach drew to a halt a short time later. The coachman had recalled his instructions perfectly. He was to stop several streets away from Thornsby's office and Robert would walk from there.

It was an unnecessary precaution, perhaps, but the habit of caution dies hard, especially as there had been times when such caution had saved Robert's life. And so he walked those last few streets alone, careful to look over his shoulder from time to time. In the doorway of the building he paused. He wished to be certain that no one was paying him any notice before he went inside.

Thornsby did not keep him waiting, but had him admitted to his office the moment he arrived. He rose as Robert entered the room.

"Well? What word do you bring me? Did you find out what was happening to the children? Did you catch the thieves stealing them away? Or was it an utter goose chase?"

Robert hesitated. It would be so easy to lie. But then Thornsby would send him back to try again to find the answers. Or worse, he would send someone else.

"I think," Robert said as he took the chair Thornsby waved him to, "you had better look at those who came forward to report the children stolen."

"What do you mean?"

"These people drove away those children. They beat them and abused them and drove them away. I do not think anyone stole the children, and I do not think anyone should take them back."

Thornsby stared at him. His eyes narrowed. "Are you telling me you failed?"

"I am telling you that I have visited each of the men who complained that their apprentices or mill workers or minors were stolen away. And in every case I found the conditions the children had been working in to be appalling and intolerable. I will have no part in returning children to such abusive masters," Robert replied, meeting Thornsby's eyes with a steady gaze.

The other man leaned back in his chair. "I see. I presume you also found the children or you would not have known to go and ask the circumstances? Nor, unless you were certain they were safe, would you stop looking because you would know that what they ran to might be worse than what they ran from."

"I know where they are," Robert agreed cautiously.

"But you do not mean to tell me?"

"I suggest again that you ask some questions of those who complained that the children were stolen from them," Robert repeated.

"By law it does not matter how they were treated," Thornsby countered.

Robert slowly rose to his feet. He leaned forward and placed his hands on Thornsby's desk. "And do you expect me to accept that?" he demanded. "Do you honestly, given what you know of my childhood, expect me to agree that it does not matter?"

Thornsby sighed. "No. And in your place I should feel the same. But I have been charged with resolving this matter, and you place me in a very difficult position."

Robert sat down again. "Why?" he asked. "Resolve the matter by writing a report stating that children would not have disappeared if they were properly treated. Report back that the children ran away. It's the truth. They were simply helped once they escaped. So write a report advising that the only way to stem the continued disappearance of these children is if their masters hadn't badly beaten them."

"You know what would be made of such a report as that. Would you be willing to give me the name of the person who helped the children after they escaped? Or tell me where they are now?"

"I will give you nothing of the sort," Robert

snapped. "You have my recommendation. And if that does not satisfy you, then you may have my resignation as well."

Thornsby frowned. "Oh, no. You shan't get off that easily. You began this case, and you will finish it."

"I will have no hand in returning children to abusive masters," Robert repeated. "Nor will I help you to do so."

"I see. And you expect me to say to these men that we cannot help them?" Thornsby asked, quirking one corner of his mouth upward.

Robert knew Thornsby very well. They had worked together for ten years. He knew better than to answer. Instead, he waited. Eventually, Thornsby sighed.

"I don't like it," he said.

"I don't like it either," Robert agreed.

"We do not mean the same thing!" Thornsby said sharply.

Robert merely waited again. Eventually, Thornsby leaned forward. "I make you no promises," he said. "Some very powerful men wish to see this matter resolved. They will not like being told that we cannot do so. Or rather that we cannot do so to their satisfaction. Where will you be when I make my decision?"

"At Henley Hall," Robert said without hesitation. And before Thornsby could ask why or express surprise, he added, "I am going to be married, and my bride is waiting for me there. You may wish me happy."

Now Thornsby gaped at him. "Married?" he echoed incredulously. "You? To whom?"

"To Henley's daughter," Robert replied with a calm he did not feel.

"When?"

"Shortly after I return. By then the last of the banns should have been read."

And then, while Thornsby was still stunned by the news, Robert rose to his feet and walked out of the room.

* * *

Alex looked up to see Margaret watching her. She was not in the best of moods. It had been weeks since Robert left and she missed him. And that made her impatient with those around her.

"You could go back to your house in the woods," Alex grumbled. "Now that Sir Robert is away on business, there is no need for you to be here to play propriety. And don't tell me that you are worried what Lady Ransley would think, for I know very well you wouldn't care. In any event, she already knows about your cottage in the woods because you showed her."

Margaret shrugged and sniffed. "Perhaps I have decided that I like it here," she said. At Alex's withering look she added, "Oh, very well. I am still here because you still need my help. No, don't look at me like that! I know very well you are starting to have doubts about this marriage. Yes, and wondering when Sir Robert will return."

Alex fingered the locket at her neck. "Margaret," she asked, "do you believe in the locket—in the legend about the faces?"

The older woman sighed. "I don't know," she said. "To be sure, there is no doubt one does see a face. I told you before, I think it must be some trick of the craftsmanship. But whether or not it is the person one is supposed to marry, I don't know. My parents would not allow your mother to marry the man whose face she saw. And I never did meet the man I saw when I looked in the locket. But my mother swore it was my father's face that she saw, and they were very happy together until the day they died."

Margaret stopped pacing about the room and sat down opposite Alex. "I don't know if the power of the locket is something real or if it is only the power of our own hearts and minds. If a woman sees a face and then a man who might be the match to that face, perhaps she looks for all the good in him, all the reasons to love and sets aside all her natural wariness and reserve. Is it surprising, then, that warmer emotions bloom?"

She paused, her voice earnest as she went on, "Does it matter if the power is real? I would rather," Margaret said, leaning forward, "see you put your faith in whether in your heart you trust Sir Robert. Whether you believe he is a good and honorable man and whether you think you can be happy married to him. Is this someone with whom you wish to spend the rest of your life?"

Alex reached out and put her hand over Margaret's. "My heart does tell me that Robert is a man to be trusted. And I do think I can be happy with him. Look at how he reacted to finding the children here. How many other men would have taken it so well?"

And what there was to trouble Margaret about that Alex could not comprehend, but troubled was the only word to apply to the older woman's expression. Still, she made an effort to smile and rise to her feet again.

In a bright voice that fooled neither of them, Margaret said, "I hope you may be right. In the meanwhile, why don't we collect the children and take them for a walk? It is a beautiful day, and they have spent far too much time cooped up inside this house the past few months. It is time they were out in the sunshine."

Tessa and Lisbeth thought it a wonderful plan, and so did Lady Ransley, who met them in the foyer. "For you must know that since Ransley discovered the stream you have is excellent for fishing he has wanted to do nothing else and I am left quite alone. I should be glad for a walk."

And so it was a rather large procession that made its way out the back door and toward the lake some distance away. The older children were laughing and running ahead. Lisbeth and Tessa ran to catch up with them. Margaret and Lady Ransley lagged behind, and Alex found herself in the middle of the rest of the children, the youngest ones who seemed to most like her company. Betsy, the maid, and Dunford, the footman, followed to the rear.

The day was bright and sunny with very few clouds in the sky. There seemed to be all the time in the world for play, and none of the adults seemed inclined to hurry inside either. Particularly as Betsy and Dunford carried baskets of food Cook had sent with them in the event they should become hungry.

"As she very well knew the children would," Margaret observed tartly. "I swear they are never satisfied!"

"They are growing," Lady Ransley replied mildly.

Margaret snorted, but she did not object when the children asked her for something from the baskets. Indeed, she smiled and seemed younger than Alex could ever recall. She wondered why her aunt had never married, never had the children she so patently would have loved. Perhaps it was Margaret for whom they ought to be seeking a husband.

As soon as the thought was formed, Alex silently laughed it away. Margaret? Married? Impossible! Who would put up with her fierce independence? Or her eccentricities?

Alex was still smiling when suddenly several men came running out from beneath a stand of trees and attempted to seize the nearest children. Immediately she was on her feet running toward them. Tessa and Lisbeth were doing the same, and behind her Alex could hear Helen and Margaret shouting.

Tessa was the first to reach one of the men. He was trying to drag James toward the trees, and Tessa began to pound on his back. He dropped the boy and pushed Tessa away so that she fell to the ground.

Now Lisbeth was pummeling a different man, one who had hold of one of the girls. He, too, let go of his captive in order to push Lisbeth away. Alex paused long enough to spy a branch that had fallen to the ground. She grabbed it and swung it at the man nearest her. She struck him between the shoulders, and he rounded on her with a roar of rage.

All three sisters and Dunford were struggling with angry men. Alex could hear Lady Ransley shouting as the maid ran toward the house for help. Somehow she knew there wouldn't be time. These men were in too much of a hurry. And they were about to get away with one or more of the children.

Suddenly Margaret's voice cut through the cries of the children and the shouts of the sisters and the curses of the men.

"Stop! Let go of the children and the women or I shall shoot!"

The man holding Alex gave an ugly laugh. "You can't shoot but one."

"Ah, but you don't know which one I shall shoot," Margaret replied. "And I warn you now that I have never missed my mark. Whomever I shoot dies."

That silenced the men. Alex managed to pull free, and she saw that her sisters had done the same. And so had the children. Everyone stood waiting.

"C'mon," the leader told the others. "T'ain't worth being shot over."

And then the men melted away into the trees. Alex and her sisters gathered the children together just as the servants came running down from the house, led by Lord Ransley. Everyone gathered around Margaret.

"Is that . . . loaded?" Lord Ransley asked.

Margaret looked him up and down. "Would there be any point to carrying it if it wasn't?" she demanded.

"Only if you liked to bluff," he retorted, undaunted by her sharp tongue.

"Well it is loaded," Margaret said. "And I would have shot, too, if it had come to that."

"Is it true that you have never missed your mark?" Lisbeth asked in a tone of awe.

"Certainly," Lord Ransley said with a chuckle, "for

I'll be bound she's never actually shot the thing so how could she have missed her mark?"

Margaret stared at him for a long, measuring moment. Then she pointed to a branch of a particular tree. Before anyone had time to stop her, Margaret shot the pistol and they all watched as the bullet smashed into the branch precisely where she had pointed. Then, with utter calm, her head held high, Margaret turned and without a word started for the house.

Wide-eyed, everyone followed, clustering protectively around the children. No one wished to risk the men returning and taking any of them away.

That's when they found that Stamford had returned from his business. They filed in through the back door and found him waiting in the foyer. He did not look pleased. Nor did Margaret, who was there with him, the pistol still in her hand, despite his obvious efforts to coax her into handing it over to him.

Alex looked at him. She wanted to throw her arms around him and ask him to hold her and keep her safe. Instead, in a voice still trembling a trifle from the shock of what had just occurred, she said, "Robert, we must talk."

Chapter 22

Lady Ransley stepped to Alex's side. "We *all* need to talk," she told Robert. Over her shoulder she said to Potter, who stood transfixed, watching everything, "I think you had best have a pot of strong tea sent up to the drawing room. And perhaps some brandy as well."

Then she started up the stairs. No one dared object, and they all followed, even the children and Betsy and Dunford as well.

"What happened?" Robert asked quietly as he walked up the stairs at Alex's side.

She told him—softly so as not to upset the children all over again. By the time they reached the drawing room, he had an appallingly clear picture of what had happened.

"They were after the children?" he asked, wanting to make certain there was no doubt.

"Unmistakably."

He took a deep breath. "Then they are not safe here and we shall have to send them away."

"No!" Her cry of protest was loud enough to draw all eyes to them. She added in a voice that was softer and meant only for him to hear, "That is, we shall take greater care to guard them! We shall keep them closer to the house! You cannot send them away."

Robert shook his head and turned toward the others. One by one, he asked the adults to give their accounts of what had occurred. The accounts tallied closely with what Alex had said.

Most of the children had been too upset to note anything useful, except for the oldest boy.

"I knew him, sir. Used ter work fer me old master, he did. Still does. He said he was here to take me back. And the other children too. Said weren't a man in England who could stop him."

"If you ran away from your master, he's right," Lord Ransley said. "He has the law on his side."

There were murmurs of protest at this blunt speaking. But it was to Robert that the boy looked, a plea for help in his eyes. And Stamford repeated what he had already said to Alex. "The children cannot stay here. No matter what you say, you cannot properly protect them here. As Lord Ransley has observed, the men have the law on their side. They acted rashly in trying to simply grab the children. But odds are, they will be back and this time with a constable in tow."

"I will not give them up!" Alex said stubbornly.

"None of us will," Margaret added. Her voice was thoughtful, however, as she looked at Robert and asked, "What would you have us do?"

"I know a place," he said. "The children would be safe and they would be happy. No one would think to connect the place with me."

"Who would care for the children?"

"And how would we get them there?"

"When would you want them to go?"

The questions continued to be flung at him, and Robert waited until they had all been asked before he tried to reply. And then he began to speak in a voice that was meant to be soothing.

"There is a couple there. I would trust them with my life. They would look after the children, for their own sake if not for mine. No one knows they know me or that I know them. So the children would be safe there. But we must send them as soon as possible, before those men can make another attempt. Early tomorrow morning, at dawn, if we can. If they go in my closed carriage with the curtains drawn, no one will know who is inside. Cook can pack them food, and my coachman can take care not to stop at any well-known posting inns. He knows how to discourage questions," he concluded grimly.

"We cannot send the children alone," Alex said thoughtfully. "One or more of us must go with them. Tessa, perhaps you and I?"

"No."

"But, Stamford—"

"No," he repeated. "Think. If the men think you are still here, they will presume the children are as well. But if you disappear, they will know something odd is happening, and they are likely to guess that you have taken the children somewhere. They will try to follow and are far more likely to find the trail if they start soon after you than if we have a week or so advantage."

"You will need our carriage as well," Lord Ransley said slowly. "There are too many children to fit into one. So it must look as if you and I and Lady Ransley have left. Hmmm, Miss Barlow, can you arrange for your servants to say in the village and to their friends that we have all left and that you and your sisters are frightened and keeping the children very close in the house?"

She nodded. It was Margaret, however, who put her finger on the flaw in the plan. "And if the men decide to attack us in the house?" she demanded tartly.

"Let out that the footmen have all been armed with cudgels and Potter with a pistol to chase off any attempts to do so," Robert answered promptly. To Alex he added, "I know this is not what you wish. But I can see no other way to make certain the children are safe. Please trust me."

She didn't want to agree, he knew it as well as he knew his own heart. But she did so anyway. "Very well. We shall have the children packed and ready before dawn."

"But who is to go with them?" Tessa asked. "You still have not told us that."

Robert hesitated. "I suppose that I could go. It is my carriage after all, and I should have to play least in sight anyway. But I much dislike leaving you alone here."

"I could go, sir, and take care of the girls," Betsy said, looking up from the corner of the drawing room, where she was engaged in keeping the youngest children calm.

"You do not mind?" he asked with a frown.

She shook her head. "I will not even mind staying there, if the couple will have me to help."

"Why?"

She looked away and then back at him. She drew in a deep breath, but could not seem to bring herself to answer. It was Dunford who answered.

"I can tell you that. There's a man. Won't leave her alone. She wants to get away from him. Let her go, sir, and take care of the girls and stay with them once they get there. And let me go, too. I'll take care of the boys." He paused, then drew in a breath himself before he said, "I'd like to marry Betsy if she'll have me. And I'm prepared to stay there and help with the children, too."

Betsy stared up at the footman, clearly as astounded as any of them by this proposal. But then he looked at her and smiled and held out a hand. Slowly, she reached out and took it. From the look on her face, there was no doubt she approved of his plan. Still Robert hesitated.

Ransley coughed. "I'd say it's an excellent notion. You'll need more than one couple to take care of all these children," he said. "Why not send the maid and footman, since they are willing to go?"

"And I should feel better if the children had someone with them they knew," Alex added.

"And it would be wise to have an adult in each carriage," Margaret chimed in.

Robert nodded. "Very well. I am grateful to you for being willing to go. But there is no coming back," he warned Betsy and Dunford, "for I want no one to be able to find the children through you."

"We understand," the footman answered, still holding Betsy's hand.

"Good. Be packed and ready tonight. I want the carriages away by the first light in the morning. Let us hope those men are not up and about until hours later."

"We shall be," Betsy answered. Then, rising to her feet she said, "Come, children, we must go upstairs and get you ready to leave."

There was sadness in their faces as the children left the room and Robert found himself wishing there was another solution. But he could see none.

Alex was still distressed. When he asked her why, she said, "I shall miss them. I think of them almost as if they were my own. I wish we could keep them here."

"Do you not understand," Lady Ransley asked in a very careful voice, "what a disservice you would be doing these children if you continued to raise them in your own home? Partly you treat them as if they were young ladies and gentlemen. And partly you teach them to hide when others are here. How are they to understand who they are, what their role in life must be?"

"You don't understand!" Alex retorted.

She looked to her aunt for support, and Margaret took a moment before she spoke. Then she chose her words with as great care as Lady Ransley had done.

"I know you care. Indeed, I care as well, and I have encouraged you to do so. But I have begun to wonder if we have been altogether wise in what we have done with the children."

"What do you mean?"

Margaret hesitated. "We have been selfish, you and I, thinking of the pleasure it has given us to rescue

these children. But Lady Ransley has a point about
how hard their future will be if they are raised as we
have been doing. They are not gentlemen or ladies,
and the *ton* would never accept them as such. But
neither are we teaching them any other skills or
expectations."

"She is right," Robert said, and he did not trouble
to hide the bitterness in his voice. "I, of all people,
know the truth of that."

"You mean that we are raising them in such a way
as must make them dissatisfied with the life they will
inevitably lead, don't you?" Tessa asked.

"Yes."

Lady Ransley reached out and took Alex's hand.
"It is good of you to care and one of the reasons
Stamford must love you. But one must listen to one's
head as well as one's heart in order to choose what is
best for those around us, whether it be children or the
man we love."

Alex's own voice was scarcely above a whisper as
she tried to answer. "I would have explained all of
this to the children when they were older, when they
were better able to comprehend such things."

"Would you?" Robert pressed her, his voice harsh
and unyielding. "And what if they had already grown
accustomed to this way of life? Already come to think
of such surroundings as their right? Already learned
to ape the manners of you and your sisters so that
their own fellows mock them for putting on airs? Or
did you hope to train them up as servants and find
them all posts when they were grown? It would not
have answered, you know. The ladies and gentlemen
of the *ton* wish for conformity from their servants
above all else, and they would not like, would not
accept, the notions your children, as you have called
them, would by then have taken into their heads."

When he paused, Margaret took up the thread.
"They will be far safer if they live quietly as Sir Robert intends, than if they are in public view, as they

inevitably would be if they lived with you. Tongues would forever be talking of them, and sooner or later others would come for the children we are trying so hard to protect."

Alex shivered. "I know you are right," she said. "But you cannot ask me to like it!"

She fled the room, and not a one of them tried to stop her. Instead, Robert went to the library to write the letter he must send with the children to the couple who would care for them. It was a fortunate circumstance that he had already stopped to speak with them when he was traveling about these past two weeks. They would not be taken entirely by surprise. But still he needed to write them a letter and enclose with it funds for the support of the children.

What they were saying in the drawing room he neither knew nor cared. The only opinion that mattered, Alex's, was only too clear. She would come around, he told himself. She had to, for he didn't know what he would do if she did not.

Chapter 23

At dawn the next morning it was a silent, sober group that gathered to help the children into the carriages and see them off. There were hugs to be given and tears to be wept, but silently and without causing any delay. Everyone present, right down to the smallest child, understood the urgency of what they were doing. Not a one wished to be taken back to the circumstances from which they had escaped.

So in the morning mist, Robert stood, his arm around Alex's shoulders, as they watched the carriages pull away to begin the journey.

"They will be fine," he told her. "They will be safe and happy."

She looked up at him. "I know," she whispered. "I just hate the necessity of doing this!"

He nodded. "Come inside. It's cold out here, and even if the children were looking out the windows of the carriages, they could no longer see you. Come inside and have some breakfast. I know you did not eat before, for you were too busy feeding the children and making certain they had what they needed for their journey. Now it is your turn."

She did not protest. Her sisters and Margaret were silent at her side. Lord and Lady Ransley had not yet come downstairs, indeed, not having the same invested interest in the children, they were almost certainly still asleep, and for that Alex was grateful. For all she knew that Helen was right in what she had said the day before, she did not wish to face that truth just now, nor the woman who had spoken it.

Robert coaxed her with toast and tea and even made her laugh at a silly story about his own youth. It was only when he was satisfied that she had taken at least a little nourishment that he turned the talk to another important matter.

"What day have you fixed for our wedding?"

"I . . . well, that is to say, I didn't because I didn't know what day you would return," Alex replied. "What day do you wish to be married?"

"The day after my carriage returns," he said promptly. "You had best go and speak with the vicar today. But take a strong footman or groom with you. I don't wish anyone to try to take you in order to get the children. No one will wonder at such caution after yesterday."

She nodded. "Of course."

"You do still wish to marry me?" he asked, a trifle anxious.

"Yes, I do." She paused and looked down and then at him. "You need a wife. And you are willing to take charge of the children and their welfare."

He dropped her hands. "I see. So you are going to marry me only for the sake of the children? I would have taken care of them anyway, you know."

"No."

He looked at her, puzzled. She smiled and touched his cheek. "No, I am not going to marry you simply for the sake of the children. Don't you understand? I want to marry you. It is true that we scarcely know each other, but I feel in my heart you are a good and honorable man."

She paused and drew a breath. With her hand, not even aware she did so, she clutched the locket at her throat. "I do not know what has caused me to forget all my vows never to marry. Or why I do not fear you as I have heretofore feared other men. I only know that I want to be with you, want to be your wife, want to love and trust in a way that I never have before."

Without a word, for it was obvious he could not bring himself to speak, Robert drew her into his arms, oblivious to the presence of the very interested servants. As he held her close, he murmured to the top of her head, "I swear I shall find a way to make you happy!"

The wedding, several days later, was a blur and yet every moment perfectly clear. Or so it seemed to Robert. At his side, Alexandra seemed both terrified and certain of her responses. And that echoed his own emotions. At her throat the locket seemed almost to glow in the sunlight that came through the window behind the altar, and Robert took an odd comfort in that, though he could not have said why.

Afterward, there was a hurried wedding breakfast, and then he and Alexandra and Lord and Lady Ransley climbed into their carriages to leave for London. When they were alone, Robert felt the need to apologize for his haste. He could not tell her about Thornsby, of course, but once again the Prince of Wales and the story they had concocted with his help served as sufficient explanation.

"The Season is almost over, and you must be presented to the *ton* before then," he told her.

"I am in mourning," she reminded him.

"The *ton* will come to call," he predicted. "They will see and approve of you."

"Will they?"

Robert squeezed her hand. "You will like London," he predicted, "and London will adore you!"

"They did not do so before," she warned.

"Ah," he said playfully, "but that was before. This is now. You are a grown woman with poise and beauty and a fortune to your credit."

She snorted in disbelief, but Robert only smiled the more and drew her hand to tuck it into his elbow.

"We shall make a very successful couple, you shall see," he predicted. "Tell me in a week if you do not find London wonderful."

She shook her head, but there was a shy smile, too—one that made him want to tilt up her chin and kiss her. With a start of surprise, Robert realized there was no reason he should not do so. He gently removed her bonnet, having discovered in the past that it would interfere with what he wished to do, and stroked her hair, then cupped her face with both hands.

"I am the most fortunate man alive!" he told her.

He resisted the impulse no longer. He bent forward and kissed his wife. Her lips parted under his, and he felt her hands steal up to grasp his shoulders. She did not draw away. Indeed, there was an untutored eagerness to her response that made Robert deepen the kiss.

When finally he let her go, their breath came much more quickly than before, and she stared at him with a look of dazed wonder in her eyes.

"I . . . I think I shall like being married," she managed to whisper.

He could not help himself—he laughed and drew her into a fiercely possessive embrace. He could not explain the joy he felt, the humble pride, when she tucked her head under his chin and snuggled against his breast as though it were the safest place in the world for her.

Had anyone ever looked to him for such comfort before? If so, Robert could not recall it. Nor known such a sense of fierce protectiveness. He would not let her be hurt, he vowed, no matter what might come.

Robert began to stroke Alexandra's shoulder, to play with the tendrils of her hair, to smile at the thought that she was his, now and forever, and he was the luckiest man on earth.

Alex was all too aware of the gentle hand stroking her shoulder, comforting her and rousing feelings within she had never known before. She wanted more, and she wanted things she could not name, but she knew somehow that Robert could give them to her.

As his hand continued to stroke her in ever wider circles, she felt a warmth spread all through her. He ought not, she was sure, to touch her there, in between her breasts at the top of her gown. And yet they were married, so perhaps it was proper after all. No one had ever thought to tell Alex what precisely it was that went on between men and women once they were married. Margaret would only say it felt much too good to be right or proper!

Well, it certainly felt good to have his fingers dip below the top of her gown and fondle each breast in turn. Nor could she say she disliked when his other hand began to stroke her legs, moving ever closer to that place between them that almost seemed to beg for his touch.

She might have objected when he lifted the skirt of her gown to reach for bare skin beneath, but when she opened her mouth to do so, he covered it with his own and kissed her so that she soon forgot whatever it was she meant to say. Who knows how far things might have gone if the carriage had not suddenly drawn to a halt and her husband hastily smoothed down her skirt and readjusted her bodice. Alex certainly would not have had the presence of mind to do so.

"What the devil is the matter?" Stamford demanded as the carriage door opened.

Lady Ransley smiled at him, not in the least daunted. "I wish to spend some time with your wife," she said with a disarming smile.

"It is my wedding day, and I prefer to ride with her," Robert countered.

Lady Ransley only smiled even more broadly. "You will have plenty of time to show her the pleasures of marriage tonight, Sir Robert. Do not be greedy. It occurred to me that your wife might wish to know a little of what to expect in London and whom she is likely to encounter. Who must be ignored and who flattered and all manner of things men generally never bother their heads about, but which are of the utmost importance to the acceptance of a lady."

He grumbled in a way that was very gratifying to Alex. Still he climbed down and let Lady Ransley take his place. The door closed, and soon they were on their way again.

Lady Ransley regarded Alex with what looked suspiciously like amusement in her eyes. Still, she was demurely respectful as she began to speak.

"Yes, I think you and Sir Robert will deal quite well together. An excellent thing given how hastily the two of you were wed. But this way the *ton* will see that it truly is a love match, and they will forgive both of you a great deal on that score alone."

"Perhaps," Alex said in as calm a voice as she could manage, "it would be best if you tell me what it is you believe I ought to know when we reach London."

Lady Ransley was not in the least offended by the setdown. Indeed, she laughed good-naturedly and set to providing the instruction that would be, she said, so important to Alex's chances of success. And Sir Robert's.

"For you must never forget that his acceptance in the *ton* is tied to yours," Lady Ransley warned. "He may have the funds, but it is your lineage that will make him acceptable in a way that he never has been before."

"I understand," Alex said.

And she did. Even in the middle of nowhere, she knew the power of society's approval or disapproval. It was the latter that had driven her father to finally kill himself, and that was a lesson one could never forget.

So she bent herself to the task of learning everything Lady Ransley could teach her. It was not as if she had never known these things, after all. Mama had begun early to teach her daughters the rules of the *ton*. And Papa, when he had brought her to London, had been determined that she do nothing to ruin her chances.

But there were new people to know about, rules to be reminded of, some things no one had ever thought to tell her. And Alex listened to all of it avidly.

Chapter 24

The *ton* chose to embrace Sir Robert Stamford and his wife. Perhaps because they knew he had been told he must marry, it was not seen as an attempt to climb the social ranks so much as a reluctant step taken out of direst necessity. His choice of bride was seen as an attempt to make amends for causing her father's death.

The ladies, in particular, made a point to take up Alexandra as though, by doing so, they could say to Sir Robert that he had been served his just deserts and that it was she they felt sorry for as well as the dire straits that had caused her to accept such an alliance.

And Alex was happy. For the first time since her mother's death, and perhaps even for some time before that, she was truly happy. In private, Robert was a loving, a very passionately loving, husband. And in public he was a dutiful one, talking as if he was truly proud of her. She could not help but contrast her appearance this time in London with the last time. If only her sisters and the children could be with her, her pleasure would be complete.

Robert was equally happy. He found doors open to him as a married man that had been firmly closed before. And he was once again in the Prince of Wales's good graces. That, however, was something he no longer trusted, and he found himself avoiding, rather than seeking out, his company.

Though he had married in haste, he felt not the

slightest reason to repent. Indeed, each day he found himself more and more grateful that fate had cast Alexandra in his way and that she had consented to marry him. There was a passion beneath her calm surface, and it flowered at his touch. The marriage bed, which might have been a duty or mere physical release, became a place that drew them ever closer— a place where they laughed together and shared more of themselves than either had ever thought possible.

Perhaps that's why, when trouble came, it came as such a shock to both of them.

They'd been in London almost three weeks. The Season was officially over, but many ladies and gentlemen still lingered. As Robert had predicted, when the *ton* realized Alex was in mourning and could not come to them, they came to call upon her. She had not had one quiet day since the *ton* learned of their presence in town. Sir Robert and Lady Stamford were too promising a subject for gossip to allow to languish by themselves!

Alex's one source of respite was to go walking in Hyde Park in the afternoons. On this particular afternoon Robert went with her. It was a bright, sunny day, and all the members of the *ton* still in London, it seemed, were out and about as well, though most of them were in their carriages—including the Prince of Wales.

He spied Robert and signaled that he should approach the prince's carriage. Alex dipped a curtsey and Robert bowed.

"Well, well, so this is your bride," Prinny told Robert approvingly. "You did very well for yourself. Very well, indeed."

"Thank you, Your Highness," Robert replied.

Prinny turned to Alex. "And you, my dear. A hero for a husband. Helping us out right now with this little intrigue of children being stolen from their rightful masters. Don't know the details, of course. All very confidential I'm told. But they say the case will be solved very soon. You must be very proud of him."

Alex felt as though she had been turned to stone. But the Prince of Wales was waiting for her to say something, and one could not ignore Prinny. In a voice that sounded as dazed as she felt, she said, "Indeed, my husband is a man of many surprises."

Satisfied that he had bestowed his approval on the couple, the Prince of Wales signaled his coachman to go on. Robert and Alex stepped back off the carriage path and watched him go. Beside her, Alex knew Robert was saying her name, but she did not want to hear what else he might want to say. Indeed, she could scarcely bear to look at him. But she had to know the truth.

"What did he mean?" she asked. "How does he know about the children?"

She could see him brace himself to answer. And that, as much as the words he said, told her what she had feared to know. Still, she let him draw her a little away so that they might have some privacy.

"I work for a man who sent me out to find some missing children. Children I had been told were stolen and being sent to the village near you."

"Why didn't you tell me?"

"I didn't know what you would do. Or what I would need to do about the children," Robert told her. "That was where I was before the wedding, visiting the men from whom the children escaped, and speaking to the man who set me on their trail."

"I see. The Prince of Wales, he said you will solve the matter soon. How are you going to do that? By returning the children to their masters?" she asked.

"No."

"Then why is Prinny so pleased with you? I cannot think he would approve of any other solution."

He frowned, and Alexandra waited, hoping and even praying that he would have an answer. That he would prove himself the Robert she had come to

know and love these past few weeks. She wanted so
dearly to know that the children were still safe.

But he didn't know that. His concern was that they
were drawing too many stares. So when he did speak,
it was only to say, "This is not the time nor place to
discuss the matter. Later, at home, I shall tell you all
about it."

"Why not tell me here, now? Are you afraid I shall
ruin your reputation and you may lose your newfound
acceptance with the *ton*? Or that the Prince of Wales
will cease to approve of you if he sees us fighting?"
she challenged him.

Robert went very pale. "Is that truly what you think
of me?" he asked.

He shook his head, a sadness in his eyes as if he
was disappointed in her! His words seemed to echo
that disappointment and sadness. "You do not
understand. You do not choose to understand. Or to
trust me. Very well, madam, have it as you will. But
the children are being well cared for and better than
you could have done. I have not betrayed them. As for
my standing in the *ton,* here is what I think of that!"

Before she could speak or defend herself, he turned
on his heel and walked away from her, oblivious to
all the stares, all the whispers that followed his
progress. He marched straight to where the Prince of
Wales was now sitting in his carriage, speaking with
someone else.

Alex started after him. She could not hear what he
said, but it was patently an insult, for the Prince's
anger was unmistakable. Suddenly, she saw Lord
Ransley also moving toward Prinny's carriage, Lady
Ransley trying hard to keep up with him. But already
Robert had turned and was walking away from the
Prince, just as he had walked away from her.

Lord Ransley tried to stop him. Robert shook off
the arm even as he answered sharply whatever his
friend had said. And then he was gone. Ransley
turned and saw Alex. He waited for her to reach him.

Lady Ransley smiled at her, but there was more anxiety than reassurance in her expression.

Lord Ransley offered his arm to Alex, but she walked past him to the Prince of Wales, who was staring after Robert and was unmistakably in a towering rage.

"Your husband, madam, is an uncivilized boor," he told Alex the moment she was within earshot. "I see that he has abandoned you as well as insulted me. My profound apologies that it was at my command that he decided to marry and that he chose you as his poor victim."

Alex felt more bewildered than she ever had in her life. She did not understand any of what was happening. And yet, in that moment, with Prinny glaring at her, she knew that she loved Robert and could not betray him to this man.

"I think perhaps it is my fault, Your Highness. That it is I who abandoned him. I who caused him to insult you by accusing him of caring more for your regard than for my feelings. It is I who owe you an apology."

The Prince of Wales blinked. He stared at the woman before him. "Because of you he insulted me?" the prince sputtered.

Alex wished she could sink into the floor. "Yes, and I'm very sorry. I never meant for it to happen!"

By her side Lord Ransley cleared his throat and said, "It would seem that not only did Stamford obey your command to marry, Your Royal Highness, but he actually fell in love with the woman."

"And isn't that the worst possible fate you could have imagined for him!" another voice chimed in.

"Far worse than mere marriage," a third agreed. "Imagine! being so tied to one's wife that one would destroy oneself for her."

Prinny stared at Alex. Then he turned to Lord Ransley and said, "When you see Stamford, tell him that he is to remain in London for the rest of the summer. I shall very much enjoy watching him live under the cat's paw."

And then he signaled his coachman to go on. Alex drew a deep breath and looked to Lord Ransley, a question in her eyes.

"I believe you may have salvaged matters for Stamford after all," he said quietly, "but I think we had best not press our luck. May I escort you home?"

He offered her his arm and Alex took it. Lady Ransley took his other arm, and with heads held high they hurried to where the Ransleys had left their carriage. Once they were safely on their way out of the park, the questions began.

"What the devil happened back there?" Lord Ransley asked.

"Did you have to choose a fight with Stamford in such a public place? In front of all those malicious eyes?" Lady Ransley chimed in. "It is a very good thing you managed to amuse rather than offend the Prince of Wales, but it was a very near thing, and then what would you have done?"

Alex felt close to tears. How could she explain when she did not understand any of it herself? "It was his notion, not mine, to create a scandal!" she whispered.

"And for what cause?" Lord Ransley demanded grimly.

"What does it matter?" Lady Ransley said impatiently. "The damage is done, and Lady Stamford did her best to undo it. Whether it will suffice or not depends on how the two of them behave in public over the next few days." To Alex she added, "We shall take you home and see if Sir Robert is there before you. If not, Ransley shall go and search for him in his favorite haunts."

"Thank you."

Robert was not home. But others were. Alex and Lord and Lady Ransley were greeted with the sight of bandboxes and trunks filling the foyer. A harassed major domo was trying to direct the servants to clear the area.

"No, Sir Robert has not yet returned," he replied when asked. "Don't drop that box!" he shouted at a footman. Then, to Alex he added in a voice devoid of expression, "Miss Winsham and her two nieces are in the parlor upstairs. We are attempting to prepare sufficient bedchambers to house everyone."

In spite of her distress, Alex thanked him and all but ran up the stairs. In the parlor she found Tessa and Lisbeth and Margaret sitting around a small table, drinking tea and sharing a plate of pastries. She hugged each one in turn as Lord and Lady Ransley watched, bemused, from the doorway.

After a moment Lord Ransley said, "We are not needed here. Shall we go, my dear?"

"Yes," Lady Ransley agreed.

They greeted and then took their leave of Alex's aunt and sisters. And the moment Alex was alone with them, she burst into tears. As Tessa and Lisbeth watched in horror, Margaret stroked her niece's hair.

"Tell me all about it," she said soothingly.

Alex did so, leaving out nothing. Not the closeness she had come to feel with Robert, nor her dismay at hearing that he had been working to find the children, nor her fear over what he might have done with them.

"For we don't really know, do we?" she asked Margaret. "We have only his word that they are safe. And what if he lied? What if he turned them over to the man he was working for? The Prince of Wales said that Robert had resolved the entire matter and what else could he have meant? For you know those men would not have stopped clamoring for their return! Oh, Margaret, what am I to do?"

Miss Winsham looked down at her niece and smiled. It was not a pretty smile. She looked at her other two nieces. "Out of the room!" she told them. "I don't want you to overhear what I am going to say. No, don't look affronted. I don't wish you to be able to tell anyone, even by accident, what your sister is going to do!"

They grumbled—there was no doubt that they grumbled—but Tessa and Lisbeth left the room. When they were gone, Margaret drew Alex onto the sofa beside her. The older woman's voice was brisk and sensible as she said, "There is only one thing to be done, my dear. You shall go and visit the children."

Alex blinked at her. "But no one knows where they are," she protested. "Stamford made certain of that."

A smile played about the corners of Margaret's mouth. "He thought he did," she agreed. "But I do not leave things to chance. Betsy, the maid who went with them, sent a letter to someone who sent it to someone else who, well, never mind. The point is that I know where the children are, and you are going to leave for there now. You will stay until I send for you. Or until I send Stamford to you. But you leave now."

"Now?" Alex asked.

"Now," Margaret confirmed. "Our coachman will not yet have left, for I told him to go into the kitchen and get something warm to drink. I shall go and speak to him myself. You go and pack as quickly as you can."

"But . . . but shouldn't I be here when Sir Robert comes back? To talk with him about all of this?" Alex protested.

"No." Margaret's voice was absolutely firm. "Regardless of what Stamford says, you will not truly trust him unless you have seen for yourself that the children are all right. And then, perhaps, you can let go of them."

"Let go of them?"

Margaret took her niece's hand. "You took in these children and cared for them as if they were your own. And I have been grateful for that. I would never want you to turn your back on children in need. But they are no longer in need."

She paused, then added, "I think, sometimes, that

you have clung to the children because you have been afraid of loving any man. And to love a child is wonderful, but not if it keeps you from knowing what it is to have a lover, a friend, someone to turn to in times of sorrow and times of joy. Someone who will not grow up and away from you as children always do."

"You have done the same," Alex whispered.

"I had no choice. But you do," Margaret countered. "Go and see the children. Only then can you let go of your fears and begin to truly have a marriage with Stamford. And perhaps, while you are gone, he will face some truths of his own. I shall make certain of that! Remember—stay until I send for you or send him to you. Now go upstairs and get ready. And hurry!"

Alex hesitated, then nodded. She ran upstairs even as Margaret made her way to the kitchen. The older woman congratulated herself on her foresight in having the coachman come inside to rest. He wasn't going to like being sent out again like this, but if they waited, Stamford might return and put a spoke in their plans. No, Alexandra must be away before that could happen.

Margaret was all but humming to herself as she stepped into the kitchen. Sir Robert Stamford was about to discover that one did not distress Miss Winsham's nieces—not without penalty at any rate. Perhaps she was meddling more than she ought, but clearly Alexandra and Sir Robert had both made a rare muddle of things and someone had to set it right.

Sir Robert Stamford looked around at the flickering candlelight in the gaming hell to which he had come for refuge. He listened with growing frustration to the laughing voices that surrounded him. Everyone sounded so happy, except him. He felt a loneliness greater than any he had known before. Greater than any he had thought possible. Even worse, when he looked at the men around him in this gaming hell, he found himself wondering who had bid for Alexandra.

He hoped his friends Lord and Lady Ransley had taken Alexandra home. Ransley would be worried, he thought with a grimace. And when next he saw Lady Ransley, she would be vocal in her displeasure at his abandonment of Alexandra in the park. But then how could they understand? They had never known such discord between them. Robert suddenly found the thought of their happy household more than he could bear.

He cursed Alexandra, then cursed himself even more. She had destroyed all his enjoyment of the social whirl he had once thought so important to his comfort, so important to his belief in himself. Now he had nothing by which to measure his value, nothing by which to gauge whether he was the gentleman his father would have wanted him to be.

And she had destroyed the pleasure he had thought he would feel when he told her the truth about himself and how he had assured the future of the children she cared for despite what Thornsby wished of him.

A voice suddenly intruded into his thoughts. "So this is where you went to ground, Stamford," Lord Ransley said, suddenly appearing at his side. "But you don't look very happy. Indeed, I should say the only face I have seen today more unhappy than yours is Lady Stamford's. Why don't you go back to her?"

It was fortunate Robert was not holding a glass at that moment or he would assuredly have crushed it. Instead, he clasped his hands tightly behind him before he answered.

"You are mistaken. Lady Stamford does not wish to see me. Her unhappiness is for the way I have disappointed her. Dash it all, Ransley, you must see what a mistake my marriage to her has been!"

"I have seen that she cares deeply for you and you for her. I even saw her defend you to Prinny in the park this afternoon," Ransley retorted. "Lie to anyone else you please about your feelings and hers and I shan't say a word. But don't try to pass such Banbury tales off to me, for I shan't believe them. A better matched pair I have never seen!"

Robert only snorted. He wanted to ask what Alexandra had said to Prinny. But pride would not allow him to do so. "I tell you that it is useless," he repeated. "Whatever she may have said to Prinny, Lady Stamford despises me."

Ransley studied him for some moments. When he spoke again, it was with a false carelessness that fooled neither of them. "Does she despise your efforts to help her sister, the one who wrote that fanciful tale you were telling me about? Is she angry at you for persuading that publisher to bring out her manuscript as a book? Is she angry at you for getting all your friends with children to subscribe to the first printing of that book? Surely she does not despise these things?"

"I did not tell her," Robert said stiffly.

"Why not?" Ransley demanded. "It could only have raised you in her estimation, knowing that you have had such a concern for the welfare of her sister. It would surely strengthen her affection for you. Indeed, I thought that was the reason you did it."

"I did it because Miss Theresa Barlow is a talented storyteller," Robert said curtly. "I did not tell Alexandra because I will not try to buy my wife's affections. No, give over, Ransley. There is too great a gulf between her and myself. Too great a difference in what we believe."

"Religious differences?" Ransley asked, taken aback. "Good heavens! I had no notion. Indeed, I thought you talked of having the vicar reading the banns. Why—"

"No, no, no!" Robert exclaimed in exasperation. "I meant we believe differently about other matters. She, that is to say, I . . . oh, never mind! It is quite impossible to explain and I refuse to even try!"

Ransley clapped his friend on the shoulder. "I shall not press you to tell me anything," he said. "But as your friend I will tell *you* to go home. Your wife is most concerned about your welfare."

Robert shook off the hand, feeling churlish as he did so. "I will go back when I am ready and not a moment before."

"Very well, then I shall go home to my wife."

Robert only shrugged at these words, and Ransley shook his head. "You are a fool!" he said without malice. "But most newlywed men are. I would stay with you, but my wife tells me she is going to present me with a pledge of her affection, and I do not want to leave her alone longer than I must."

Robert looked startled, then grinned. "Give my apologies to your wife for causing you to neglect her. And give her my felicitations on her interesting condition. Tell her I said she is more beautiful than ever."

Ransley shook his head. "Oh, no. Not until you are safely reconciled with your wife will I pass on your compliments to her. Good God, man, do you think I mean to risk her having her head turned by your polished ways?"

"Oh, to be sure. As though there were the least chance of that!" Robert retorted derisively. "Never mind. Go home to your wife."

The grin on Stamford's face lasted only until Lord Ransley had left the gaming hell. He liked knowing his friends were happy. It was something he envied and wished for. And until today he had hoped to find an equal happiness for himself. But clearly he had been mistaken.

Chapter 25

Alex watched the children playing. They were happy—happier than she had ever seen them, even when they were staying with her.

"Where are the two oldest?" she asked Betsy.

"Placed in a proper household nearby," the maid explained. "He's to be a groom, for he loves horses. And she's to work in the kitchen. Very proud, they were, to be hired and earning their own living. It's a good household, too. I made certain of that myself. They'll not be mistreated in any way, I promise you."

"This was the right thing to do, then?" Alex asked.

"Oh, yes, ma'am, it truly was!" Betsy answered fervently.

Alex drew in a deep breath. She owed Robert an apology. Whatever the Prince of Wales meant, he had not betrayed them. How then, she wondered, was the case to be resolved? But why had he not confided in her the truth of what he was doing? Not at first, perhaps, but later? Was it that he did not know how to trust or that he did not know how to trust *her*? And how could she help him learn?

Robert sat in the darkness, one candle lit at his elbow. He had looked everywhere, asked everyone, and still found not a trace of where Alexandra had gone. She seemed to have utterly disappeared. And he felt as if he had lost a part of himself.

He was deep into the second bottle of brandy when the library door suddenly opened. He looked up, hoping to see Alexandra. Even though she had been gone a week, every time a door opened, he hoped it would be his wife.

But it was only Margaret. Miss Winsham, he reminded himself. She was born, and always would be, a lady despite her eccentricities, of which there were many. It was a bitter thought to him that an accident of birth could mean so much, so he took another sip of brandy.

"Are you lost?" he asked, staring at his glass.

Her shrewd eyes took in his condition. "No," she said in acid tones, "I am not lost. But it looks as if you may be."

As he watched with a fascinated, if inebriated, gaze, Miss Winsham carefully closed the door behind her and advanced upon him. She looked around, chose a chair, and drew it close to his desk. He frowned.

"Not lost? What the devil do you want then?"

"To talk with you," was her cordial reply.

Robert frowned at her. "Why?"

"I am concerned about your marriage," Miss Winsham said, sitting down and eyeing him shrewdly.

Robert shook his head. "What marriage? M'wife is gone, and I haven't the faintest notion where she's gone to. Don't suppose you know?"

"Perhaps."

Hope leapt in his eyes at these words, and he leaned forward eagerly. "Where? Where is Alexandra? Is she all right?"

"No, I don't think I shall tell you just yet," Miss Winsham said, shaking her head. "At the moment I am more concerned with your condition than with hers."

"Why?"

It was curt, too curt to be polite, but at the moment Robert found it hard to care. If Miss Winsham wasn't going to tell him how to find Alexandra, then all he wanted was to be left alone to drink himself into oblivion. And that was going to be hard to do so long as she was sitting there chattering at him.

"Because, much as you may wish I would just go away and leave you to your brandy, there is something you need to hear while you are still sober enough to understand. Though I may," she said, wrinkling up her nose, "be too late for that."

"You are!" he assured her fervently. "Much too late. Not sober, not sober at all. Bosky. Three sheets to the wind. Best leave it for tomorrow. Better yet, best leave it for never!"

Robert laughed at his own jest. Miss Winsham was not amused. "You are going to listen," she said. "But perhaps after," she added, rising to her feet, "you drink the posset I am going to prepare."

That alarmed Robert, and he also tried to stand. But he was more accurate than he knew in the assessment of his condition. The room began to spin alarmingly, and he promptly sat back down again.

Ten to one, he reassured himself, he would pass out before Miss Winsham returned with whatever it was she had gone to fetch. And even if he didn't, he could certainly pretend he had, and then she would have to go away and leave him alone.

Only she didn't. When she found him slumped over his desk, apparently asleep, she decided to check his condition with the most reliable method she knew. She set down the cup she was carrying and grabbed a fistful of hair. She pulled his head upward.

"Ow! Stop that!" Robert commanded.

She instantly released his head and pushed him backward in his seat instead so that he was once again sitting upright. Then she reached for the cup and handed it to him.

"Drink!" she commanded.

Because it was easier to do so than to argue, Robert tried. He almost spit out the first mouthful and would have dumped the rest if she had not threatened him.

"You'll drink every bit of that or you will face

worse in your food. And then you'll wish you had only
had to drink a simple posset!"

Because he did not doubt her ability to do as she
promised, Robert downed the liquid, grimacing with
every mouthful. But he drank it, then set the cup on
his desk and shoved it away from him. He did not like
to have to admit he felt much better when he was
done, and so he went on the attack instead, hoping to
rout her that way.

"Now that I have drunk your posset, Miss Winsham,
what the devil are you doing in my library? I do not
recall giving you permission to come in."

She snorted. "You didn't. Wouldn't have had the
sense to do so if I bothered to rap at the door and
ask. You'd best accept right now, Sir Robert, that I
am a determined woman and I do what I wish. You
had also best accept that I generally know what's
best."

It was his turn to snort. "Unless you mean to tell
me how to find Alexandra, leave me alone," he said.
"I am neither related to you nor intimidated by your
reputation as a witch."

"You ought to be," she said, leaning forward. "Still,
you're a man and men are fools. You'll listen because
you have no other choice if you ever hope to have
me tell you how to find Alexandra. The posset should
have cleared your head by now, but you'll find you're
still too unsteady on your feet to run away from me.
Besides, I would only follow, and I have a key to every
room in this household!" she concluded triumphantly.

He didn't even try to ask how she had managed
that little trick. Perhaps Alexandra had given Miss
Winsham her set of keys. In any event, he didn't really
care. What mattered was how to get her to leave
him alone.

"Very well, tell me what you came to say and then
be done with it!" he demanded.

She leaned back in her chair and smiled grimly.
Which was fortunate. Robert did not think he could

have resisted throwing something at her if she had looked at him with any sort of glee. But she looked no more happy than he did. Even less so, if such a thing were possible.

"You are a fool. Why didn't you tell my niece how and why you gained your title and the means to support it? As it is, how can she help but think you pandered to the Prince of Wales? Or that you would betray the children without a second thought. You might ask yourself why you are so afraid to have her know you for the hero you were."

He stared at her. "You are a witch," he whispered.

Miss Winsham snorted. "A witch? No. I am sorry to disappoint you, but what you seem to see as magic is merely the ability to know what questions to ask and how to find the answers. It was not difficult to discover the truth about you, Sir Robert! I was never, after all, entirely isolated from my old acquaintances in the *ton*. When I heard you had won Henley's estate, I made it my business to learn what I could about you. When you married my niece, I asked even more questions. And when I came to London and heard what had happened in the park, I persisted until someone finally told me the truth."

Robert tried to execute a bow and failed. His choice of words mocked hers. "And *I* am sorry to disappoint *you,* but your sources were mistaken. You are wrong, completely wrong about me! I am not a hero."

"Am I mistaken?" she asked mockingly. "I do not think so. Think about what I said, Sir Robert. I should not like to think you were a complete fool and entirely past redemption. You have some choices to make—including whether or not to tell Alexandra the truth about your work for Mr. Thornsby. I hope you will make the right ones."

Miss Winsham started to rise, but Robert's voice halted her. "Alexandra is my wife," he said, his voice low and angry. "She ought to have trusted me without my having to tell her a thing. Did she think I would throw away my career just to please her? Does she wish to find herself cut by all her acquaintances? Her husband stripped of his title, lands, and fortune?"

Miss Winsham slammed her hand on the desk, causing him to jump. "You are a fool! You know how her father treated her. You ought to understand that she will care more for how she is treated than for the money a man has or whether or not he has a title. I am telling you that despite the self-doubts you had, and still might have, you have the chance to keep a good marriage with my niece. But I tell you bluntly that she will not love a man who cares more for his own advancement than in doing what is right."

She paused and sighed. "That is all I wish to say, Sir Robert. I hope, I truly hope, that you will think about it and do what is right. You might also consider the possibility that by not telling Alexandra about your work for Mr. Thornsby that you put her in danger back at Henley Hall. Because you did not tell her, she was utterly unprepared when those men tried to take back the children. And here in London, how do you know you did not put her in danger? Suppose someone assumed she knows where the children are and kidnapped her to try to find out? You called me a witch, but the only magic that I know for certain exists is in the power of love. Yes, you may stare. Who am I to say such a thing? A wizened old spinster? But simply because I have not been fortunate enough to find someone to love does not mean that I have not seen the power of love firsthand. Or know the folly of turning one's back on the real thing!"

And with that parting shot, Miss Winsham sailed out of the room. Robert stared after her until the door closed behind. Then he shook his befuddled head. Could she be right? Had something happened to Alexandra because he had not told her about Thornsby and the work he did? He was trying to protect her!

Miss Winsham said he should do what was right.

But how the devil was he supposed to be certain what that was? He thought he had been doing what was right!

Robert was tired, very tired. He thought he would lay his head down, just for a few minutes, and rest. Just a few minutes, for there were plans to make and he ought to pack if he meant to leave in the morning. Just a few minutes, that was all. Five minutes later, he was sound asleep.

That was how the servants found him in the morning when the note came from Thornsby demanding that he appear at his office within the hour.

The unexpected summons, coupled with Miss Winsham's words of the night before, had Robert fretting all the way over to Thornsby's office. What had happened now? Was Margaret right that some mishap had befallen Alex? Had Thornsby somehow found out?

Thornsby was not in the best of moods. "Sit down," he growled the moment Robert was shown in.

He glared at Stamford, but Robert knew the other man too well to do anything other than wait patiently for him to say what was going on. Finally, Thornsby did so.

"You are very fortunate, Stamford. We have been able to persuade all those men to drop their claims to those children. And warned them that if they do not improve working conditions, they are likely to lose more. But this is not the way we work, Stamford. I expect that you will not try such a thing again."

Robert stared at the man who had been his mentor for ten years. "Perhaps I should simply tender my resignation now," he said.

Thornsby shook his head. "Oh, no. I'm not about to lose the best agent I've ever had that easily. Now, about your next assignment—"

"Sorry," Robert said, rising to his feet. "I cannot take on another assignment just yet. Perhaps not at all. I was serious about my resignation."

"Here, now!" Thornsby said hastily. "Take a short break. Enjoy your new bride. Come back in a week or two and we will talk then."

Robert drew in a deep breath. "That depends," he answered.

"Upon what?"

"Upon what Alexandra says when I tell her about my work and I ask her what she thinks I ought to do."

And with that, Robert walked out of Thornsby's office. He could hear the man calling after him, but he didn't care. The only thing that mattered was that the children were safe. And he was going to find Alexandra.

He made one or two stops, including speaking to Lord and Lady Ransley. Then he went home and searched the house until he found Miss Winsham sitting in the kitchen, exchanging recipes with his cook. One look at his face, however, and she rose to her feet and followed him upstairs.

"Well?" she demanded when they were alone.

"Tell me where to find Alexandra," he said.

"Why?"

"So that I can tell her the matter of the children is resolved and they are safe and I can ask her advice as to whether to resign my position working for Thornsby or take on a new case."

For what seemed like a very long moment, Robert held his breath as he waited for her answer. Finally, she smiled and began to talk.

Chapter 26

Robert found Alex in the dairy. She was watching one of the younger girls learn to churn butter, but she turned at the sound of his footsteps. She stared at him in disbelief, and he waited for her to begin to rail at him again.

"Robert?" she asked with some uncertainty, as if she did not entirely trust what she saw.

He came forward and stopped a foot or two away. He took her hands between his and said fiercely, "I cannot, I will not lose you! If you want me to resign my work with Thornsby, I will. If you want me to come and live here with you and the children, I will. I don't know if I know how to love or how to trust or how to raise children, but I mean to try to learn."

Her hand crept up to stroke the side of his face. "And I shall help you. But I cannot take you from London," she said. "Nor ruin your chances for the life you want."

"I cannot, I will not, take my value from what others say about me. You have taught me what a hollow measure of a man that is," he answered with quiet dignity. "I once thought the respect of the *ton* was all I wanted. Now I know that it is yours I value more."

She tried to choose her words with care.

"You were right, Robert, to say that I cannot raise these children as if they were my own. And right to send them here. They are happier than I have ever seen them."

She paused and looked him in the eye, wanting him
to see that she meant what she was about to say. "I
have also been thinking about the things the Prince
of Wales said. And I realize I was foolish to believe
the words of someone I had never met before when
I know in my heart you are a good and honorable
man. I don't want you to resign from your work,
Robert! If you do, then who will do it instead? What
sort of man? One who would have returned the
children to their masters without a second thought?
Perhaps brought charges against Margaret and myself?
No, I've come to understand that it is important to
have a good and honorable man, a man like you,
working for this Thornsby, for just such occasions as
this."

Robert felt something in his throat, something that
would not let him speak. And when she touched his
arm, her face a picture of concern, it was all he could
do to whisper hoarsely, "I am the luckiest of men!"

She smiled again, more broadly now, and her hand
left his arm to steal up around his neck to draw his
head toward her. "And I am the luckiest of women,"
she said right before she pulled his head the rest of
the way for a kiss.

This was his wife. A woman he had known for a
few short weeks and yet who felt as though he had
known her an eternity. A woman with whom he would
be happy to spend an eternity. And that seemed a
miracle in itself.

The glow of warmth within him was shattered when,
after he let her go and she stepped back, she gave a
cry of dismay.

"What's wrong?" he asked, bewildered and worried.

Her face was very pale. "The locket! It's gone," she
cried. "I would swear it was around my neck a
moment ago. But then it suddenly became very warm
and now it's gone!"

They looked, but it was patently hopeless. There
was no locket to be found anywhere at the farm. In

the end, he consoled her with the promise of another, to be made to her precise instructions. And he soothed her distress with more kisses.

In London Margaret gave a start of surprise when she opened the little box that held her treasures. Carefully she lifted the familiar locket out and held it up to the sunlight. How the devil had it come to be here? she wondered. She could have sworn Alexandra was wearing it when she left London.

"Is it really magic, then?" she asked herself softly.

She sat in the nearest chair, staring at the locket in her hand. She had always told herself it was nonsense, but perhaps she was wrong. Well, if Alex did not need the locket any longer, then perhaps it was time to give it to Tessa.

Author's Note

The welfare of children and the issue of child abuse is something very close to my own heart. That's one of the reasons I wanted to create characters like Margaret and Alexandra, who would care so deeply.

I also want to let you know that this is the first in a series of three books about the Barlow sisters. Look for Tessa's story next, in *The Widower's Folly*. What happens when this talented teller of tales meets a widower and his only daughter, a child who has withdrawn from the world but loves the stories Tessa creates?

Look for news of upcoming books at my Web site: http://www.sff.net/people/april.kihlstrom.

I love hearing from readers. I can be reached by e-mail at: april.kihlstrom@sff.net

Or write to me at: April Kihlstrom
PMB 240
532 Old Marlton Pike
Cherry Hill, NJ 08053

Please send an SASE for a newsletter and reply.